A Lasting Love Affair

Darcy & Elizabeth

P. O. Dixon

A Lasting Love Affair: Darcy and Elizabeth

ISBN-13: 978-1494474072
ISBN-10: 1494474077

To my beautiful daughter,
Elizabeth

Acknowledgments

Having borrowed the beloved characters as well as many of my favorite passages from *Pride and Prejudice*, I bestow my sincerest gratitude to Miss Jane Austen. What a difference my life is because of her.

Table of Contents

"Give a girl an education and introduce her properly into the world, and ten to one but she has the means of settling well, without further expense to anybody."

Jane Austen

Chapter 1

The Rule of Other's

March, 1813

Elizabeth busied about the room arranging her belongings. With her maid, Betsy, out of the way, Elizabeth was at liberty to arrange her things as she saw fit. She had to admit it was a remarkably pretty apartment of a nice, comfortable size—a corner room with windows on two sides. On one side, she could look across the lawn behind the house to a beautiful hanging wood, and on the other, she beheld a view of fine bold hills. As much as she relished being out of doors, the thing she considered most important, ironically, was the writing desk situated in front of one window. Elizabeth was sure to enjoy her most pleasurable moments sitting there. On the whole, she had no cause at all to repine about the room; its greatest failing being it simply was not home. She placed her favourite books on the shelves and hung her sister's drawings on the walls. Resting her hands on her hips, she studied her surroundings. *This apartment is going to be mine for the unforeseeable future. I had best accustom myself to it.*

Elizabeth's father, Mr. Thomas Bennet of Longbourn in Hertfordshire, had the best of intentions in sending her there. In consenting to have her stay with her aunt and his estranged elder sister, Lady Vanessa Barrett, he had afforded the means of healing the breach in his family—a breach that had commenced on the day he chose Miss Fanny Gardiner as his bride.

When Elizabeth allowed herself to think through the arrangement she had agreed to enter on the bequest of her dear father, she began to see that it was for her own benefit as well. The past year and a half had been the most difficult stretch of Elizabeth's life. Day after day, night after night, one interminable week after another, and Elizabeth's spirits still faltered. Having prided herself for so long on her philosophy of thinking only of the past as its remembrance gave her pleasure, even she did not recognise herself.

Now here she was entering a new period of her life under the stewardship of a woman whose acquaintance she had not yet made, for her ladyship was in the village attending the poor and less fortunate when Elizabeth's carriage arrived. Elizabeth had been impressed by the warm reception she received, nevertheless, even though it was made clear to her that an introduction to her aunt would occur at dinner and not a moment before.

She called out in response to the knock on her door. In waltzed Betsy. "Her ladyship asked me to look in on you and see if there is anything you need. I'm to inform you that dinner is promptly at five."

Amused, Elizabeth smiled. Punctuality must surely be the rule in her aunt's establishment. *I wonder what other rules I must abide.* "Thank you, Betsy. I have all that I require, and I believe I have sufficient time to prepare. It is only three o'clock."

"I am only doing as I was told. I meant no offence."

"I took no offence, I assure you," Elizabeth voiced in a more appeasing tone.

Betsy wandered over to the wardrobe and went about the business of looking through Elizabeth's things—what little there was. Elizabeth was not used to the notion of having her own maid. At home in Hertfordshire, she and her sisters had shared a single maid. *Something else to which I must accustom myself, I suppose.*

Elizabeth discerned the fine tailoring of her maid's dress—far richer than the gowns Elizabeth owned. She joined Betsy's side. "There is not much to choose from. I fear my aunt will be disappointed."

"She might—but she has made an appointment for you at her modiste. In no time at all, your wardrobe will be quite up to her expectations."

"Yes, Lady Vanessa's generosity is boundless." Elizabeth reflected upon her mode of travel in the fine private coach as well as all her family's astonishment that Lady Vanessa had sent Betsy to Hertfordshire to accompany her on the long journey. Elizabeth pulled out the dark-brown gown and the pale-green one, and she walked over and arranged them on the bed. She picked up the first one. "Which shall it be, Betsy? Will it be this one?" She held the dress before her. Before Betsy mustered a reply, Elizabeth held up the second gown. "Or will it be this one?"

The golden-haired young woman, who looked but a couple years older than Elizabeth, pursed her lips.

Elizabeth tossed the gown aside and plopped down on the bed. "I shall decide later. Now I believe I shall take a walk. It is such a lovely day."

Betsy gathered the two discarded garments and placed them where they belonged. "Then I will return to attend you in an hour if that is agreeable."

Elizabeth nodded, and soon Betsy was gone. Her purpose in sending Betsy on her way accomplished, she was finally at leisure to do the one thing that satisfied her more than anything else: capture her thoughts in a missive to her dearly beloved sister, Jane. Afterwards, there would be time enough for her escape from the manor house for a brisk stroll about the lovely grounds, which she credited as being, by far, the finest she ever recalled seeing. The grounds alone were enough to spur enthusiasm over her new life.

She settled comfortably at her desk and began writing where she had earlier left off.

> The first part of my journey was suffered in too much melancholy over the prospect of my leaving my beloved Longbourn to occasion any measure of pleasantness. But as I drew towards the end of it and beheld the magnificence of the country I am to inhabit for the indeterminate future, I began to appreciate my fate—to be the means of healing the breach between my father and his sister, to reside with her here in Bosley, and to be the heir apparent to all her worldly possessions pursuant to my fulfilling her expectations of all that her niece and heir ought to be.

Elizabeth was two pages into the recitation of her journey from Hertfordshire—the comfort of the carriage, the condition of the roads, and the inns she had patronised—when a light rap on the door stole her concentration. She glanced at the clock on the mantelpiece. *Where has the time gone? Pray it is not Betsy.* Elizabeth went to the door and opened it. "Betsy."

The young woman curtsied and proceeded quickly into the room. "Miss Elizabeth, I've come to help you prepare for dinner, if I may."

"Yes, I do not believe it can be put off any longer."

After dinner, Lady Vanessa sat in the parlour with her niece. Elizabeth was telling her aunt about her sister. "Jane always said the world was bright and good. I cannot recall a time when she ever spoke ill of anyone."

Having been rendered completely aghast upon seeing her niece for the first time, Lady Vanessa continued to observe Elizabeth with a critical eye. She supposed she had her work cut out for her in light of the circumstances of her niece's upbringing. *What does the daughter of a tradesman know about rearing a gentlewoman?*

Although her clothing was completely unremarkable, one's eyes were drawn to her golden brooch, which was quite lovely as best Lady Vanessa could tell from a distance of only a few feet. The years had taken quite a toll on her ladyship's beauty as well as her eyes. She did not intend to serve as nature's accomplice by wearing spectacles. Her ladyship thought Elizabeth's skin was rather brown, even a bit coarse—a consequence of her recent travels, no doubt. *However, Betsy and she travelled under the same circumstances. I detected no such alteration in Betsy.* Not everything she observed was met with displeasure. *Elizabeth's hair is perfectly arranged. I suppose I have Betsy to thank for that.*

She talks incessantly of her sister Jane. She misses her very much, I am sure.

"I understand your sister Jane's place in your heart shall forever be the most cherished. No doubt you miss her dearly, but what of your other sisters? I should love to hear more about them, as well. Of course, my brother proclaims them to be the silliest girls in England, but he has always countenanced such opinions about the fairer sex—at least for as long as I can recall."

"My sister Mary, who is next to me, is best described as a young lady of deep reflection. She is an ardent reader, and she is most proud of her accomplishments on the pianoforte. When she is not reading, she is practising."

"It sounds as though your sister Mary is a very accomplished young woman. The constant improvement in one's mind through the practice of reading is a laudable quality."

Elizabeth accepted the compliment on behalf of her sister and recommended speaking. "Kitty is next to Mary."

"Kitty?"

"Pardon, your ladyship, for you likely have heard her spoken of by her given name, Catherine. My youngest sister, Lydia, can be credited for calling her 'Kitty' I suppose by insisting as a young child that she was more like a kitten than a cat." Elizabeth chuckled, likely in recollection of the childhood memory, but Lady Vanessa was not amused.

Her ladyship raised her eyebrows and laced her voice with condescension. "I suppose one would have had to be there to appreciate the story."

Elizabeth cleared her throat. "I suppose you are correct, your ladyship." Elizabeth went on to describe her two younger sisters. By her niece's account, Lady Vanessa considered that perhaps her brother was correct, for try as Elizabeth might to extol their antics with consideration and affection, her ladyship could not but suppose that indeed they *were* rather silly.

Fortunately, the same cannot be said of Elizabeth. My brother once said his second eldest had something more of quickness than her sisters. That was long ago when he had been the one to attempt reconciliation, but Lady Vanessa had not been inclined to agree. She had her principles, and certain rules of society absolutely must be upheld for the protection of the greater good. The prospect of dying alone with no one of her own blood to give a care obliged her to alter her opinion.

Elizabeth's later mentioning of her youngest sister's fast friendship with the bride of the colonel of the militia and her ardent wish that she would be invited to go with the couple to Brighton when the militia decamped later in the spring, drew Lady Vanessa's attention and, by her tone, her disapprobation.

"Brighton? Will your mother accompany her?"

"No. Should Papa consent to the scheme, the colonel shall be charged with Lydia's supervision. Papa is convinced she will meet with no harm owing to her lack of fortune and relatively insignificance in comparison to the older, more accomplished women available to divert the officers."

"I take it you have reservations?"

"Lydia is young and impetuous, and she is a very deter-mined flirt. She is bound to make herself ridiculous wherever she goes. A young girl of her temperament is likely to attract a fair amount of mischief. But Papa insists that there shall be no peace at Longbourn if Lydia does not go to Brighton. For that reason alone, I fear he will consent to the scheme."

As much as she was disheartened over the prospect, Eliza-beth had chosen to leave the matter at that. She had done her best to persuade her father, and there was nothing more to do. Besides, it would be many weeks before a final decision was needed. Having had so little contact with any of the officers herself, save a Lieutenant George Wickham with whom she delighted in a brief discourse, Elizabeth supposed she was being overly concerned. *Were all the officers nearly so agreea-ble, there truly would be no cause for apprehension.*

"I know none of the particulars, and yet, I am inclined to agree with you. However, on the matter of your sisters' lack of fortune, your father has no one to blame for that unhappy circumstance save himself. It is most disturbing to me that my brother has done nothing to break the entail on Longbourn, relying instead on his wife to give birth to a male. Has your family even met the young man who is to inherit the estate—a Mr. William Collins, I believe?" She huffed. "I understand he has been granted a living in Kent."

"Yes, Mr. Collins visited Longbourn last autumn."

"No doubt he meant to take stock of his birth right. Is he married, or is he single? For if he is single then perhaps he might marry one of your sisters, thereby acquitting my brother, Thomas, from the shame of his lapse."

"Mr. Collins was single when he arrived, but he has since married." Clutching her brooch, Elizabeth diverted her eyes away from her aunt. "He is married to a dear friend of mine: the former Charlotte Lucas from a neighbouring village—Lucas Lodge."

"Lucas Lodge—a neighbouring estate of Longbourn? I have never heard of the place." Her ladyship pursed her lips. Racking her brain, she recalled a Mr. William Lucas who had been in trade in Meryton. *Oh, yes! He had made a tolerable fortune and had risen to the honour of knighthood by an address to the king during his mayoralty.* "Has William Lucas—or should I say, has *Sir* William Lucas gone and fancied himself a landowner—a gentleman of breeding—rather than the tradesman that he is by virtue of his father and his father's father?"

"I know not how to answer your ladyship without casting aspersions on my dear friend and acquaintances from home. There is no shame in what he has done."

"You speak your mind most decidedly for one who is so young. After what your father has done in marrying beneath his sphere, I supposed I cannot fault you for failing to recognise the differences amongst society's ranks, but as you are a gentleman's daughter, you must learn to appreciate the distinctions. *I* mean to make certain that you do."

Elizabeth had no doubt of the veracity of her aunt's pronouncement. By now she had stopped studying her ladyship's countenance for similarities to her father and sisters, for she had discerned quite enough to satisfy her curiosity. Never had she met anyone who stated her opinion so unreservedly, regardless of the person's age. *Lydia, perhaps,* Elizabeth considered, fighting desperately to subdue her amusement. It is most fortuitous that her ladyship was distracted by Sir Lucas's elevated rank, else she would have seized upon the fact that someone other than a Bennet daughter had landed the hand of Longbourn's heir. *One can only imagine what she might say if she learned that I had been the means of Mr. Collins's asking for my friend's hand in marriage by virtue of my spurning his offer.*

Her ladyship's voice pierced Elizabeth's musings. "I shall require you to attend the horse racing contest with me later in the week, Elizabeth. Several of the local gentry mean to pit their finest bays against one another."

Elizabeth frowned. "A race, your ladyship?"

"Indeed. Everyone who is anyone will be in attendance. People come from miles away." Widening her eyes, she placed her jewellery-laden hand to her chest. "Surely you are no stranger to the sport. Attending the races throughout the country was one of my dear husband's favourite pastimes. Your father must have taken his family to enjoy the races."

"My papa does not relish games of chance or high-stakes gambling, which in my limited understanding is largely the basis of horse racing. Hence, my family has never celebrated the sport."

"It is a shame; however, I cannot pretend to be surprised. Horse racing is the sport of a gentleman, and your father practically forfeited his claim to such a distinction when he married the daughter of a tradesman."

Steel infused Elizabeth's spine. "Pardon me, your ladyship. I am aware of the gulf between you and my father as well as the purpose of my being here as your way of healing the breach. However, you cannot expect me to countenance your repeated insults against my family. I cannot and I will not."

"Once again, you insist upon voicing such strong, unreserved opinions. You will learn that I speak my mind with equal enthusiasm." Furrowing her brow, she looked Elizabeth straight in the eye. "I can see our alliance shall be mutually advantageous, for I shall endeavour to temper my sentiments, and you, young lady, shall learn to temper your insolence."

Elizabeth had no interest in attending the race; however, she had nothing better to do. If what her aunt said was true about everyone being there, then it would provide a chance to meet people of her own age. If she had to spend many nights suffering her current circumstances, it would be a long, arduous stay indeed.

Elizabeth rose and walked across the room to garner a more advantageous view of her aunt's pianoforte.

"Do you play, Elizabeth?"

Before she could respond, her ladyship repined on how long it had been since she was last afforded a chance to enjoy an exhibit on the grand instrument in her home. The pianoforte had been a gift from her deceased husband, Sir Frederick Barrett, and she had played extremely well by her own account. Her fondness for playing had diminished in concert with his passing. What a delight it would be to once again witness the occasions of the room being filled with music.

Elizabeth saw no point in contesting. Exhibiting for her aunt would give her just as much pleasure as it would afford her relation, for it would serve as a pleasant alternative to her discourse, which bordered on offensive. Elizabeth went through the chief of the sheet music arranged before her, and soon her ladyship announced her intention of retiring for the evening.

Glad to have survived the evening unscathed save a few slightly bruised feelings suffered on behalf of her relations, Elizabeth sat at her desk and took out her missive. Writing in the late evening hours was a habit she had cultivated many months ago. She found it far more settling to write whenever she felt compelled to, which was frequently of late—ever since her father shared the happy news that his sister had written to him, extended an olive branch, and announced her intention to take Elizabeth under her wing.

Both of Elizabeth's parents had every reason to agree to the scheme. Mr. Bennet agreed because nothing would please him more than to see his favourite daughter so well situated in life, even though he would find himself with no one to add sensibility to the evening conversations. Mrs. Bennet was satisfied knowing she had one fewer daughter for whom to find a husband. Her words resounded in Elizabeth's ear: *Why should your father's sister not shoulder that burden when she is so very rich and living in that fine estate in Bosley, and she has no children of her own?*

Elizabeth mended her pen while nursing her busy thoughts. Her aunt truly was something else. Elizabeth could hardly wait to scribble her suppressed sentiments on paper. Her pen repaired, Elizabeth started writing where she left off before dinner.

> I now comprehend why Mama and Papa spoke
> little of Lady Vanessa while we were growing up, es-

pecially Mama. Her ladyship does not have a kind word to say about our mother. She blames her for Papa's general failure to exercise better stewardship of Longbourn; thereby enhancing rather than depleting its coffers. Her ladyship affirms that had Papa not married beneath him—to a tradesman's daughter— he might have chosen a woman from his own sphere—a gentleman's daughter with a decent dowry.

Her ladyship did not bother to curb her dismay when the result of her extensive inquisition yielded such a bountiful harvest of mortification. "Is it any wonder the five of you were reared in a household with no governess, one maid between you, and no benefit of the masters," were but some of her hearty declarations. Clearly she does not know her brother at all to suppose he would have taken us to Town to study with the masters. Perhaps she knows him all too well, and his dislike of Town is a recently acquired distaste—perchance a result of his unequal alliance. Pray forget I said that, and owe it to her ladyship's unrelenting haranguing of Mama's family legacy.

I have been here only one day, and it seems as if I have been here for a week! Her ladyship's inspection is brutal, and she has a very keen eye. I have no wish to be impertinent, but I fear if I do not, I shall grow afraid of her. That would never do, especially as I am to be her heir apparent, and all I have to do is live with her here in splendour until she makes it official.

Elizabeth looked up when Betsy entered the room. "I came to help you prepare for bed, Miss Elizabeth." She started turning down the bed covers. "Is that a letter you are writing? I'll carry it down and place it with the other letters for the post if you'd like."

Elizabeth slid the paper into her desk and turned the key. "No—that is quite unnecessary, Betsy."

"It is no trouble. I shall be delighted to be of service to you."

"No!"

Lowering her eyes, Betsy bit her bottom lip "I only mean to help." After a moment, she retrieved Elizabeth's nightgown from the drawer and laid it on the bed. "Did you enjoy your evening with her ladyship?"

What was Elizabeth to say? She could not very well tell her maid that she found her ladyship's manner to be rude, dicta-torial, and off-putting. She had only met Betsy a few days prior at Longbourn when she arrived to accompany Elizabeth on the journey to Bosley. Her new maid might well be a spy for all she knew. She fancied her aunt as just the type of iron-fisted ruler who would want to know everything that was taking place in her home. Wanting to say something to her aunt's credit, Eliza-beth reflected back to the dinner table heavily laden with platters of meats, vegetable dishes, assorted fruit, and fine wines, prepared solely for the two of them.

She nodded. "Dinner was superb."

"I shall pass your compliments on to the cook and to her ladyship as well." She clasped her hands. "Oh, just wait until you learn what her ladyship has in store for you tomorrow."

Elizabeth pursed her lips in wonderment. She retrieved the key from her drawer and clutched it tighter. *If she presumes to report back to her ladyship on a compliment as innocuous as my sentiments on the meal, then I shall suppose Betsy is a spy!*

A Lady's Imagination

"Pardon me, Miss—" The tall, striking gentleman immediately knelt before Elizabeth, and one by one he handed her the toppled parcels and books scattered about on the ground. Amazed at finding herself in such a position even though she saw it coming but had been unable to avoid it, she accepted the packages in silence.

He stood and cleared his throat. "I understand it is the established mode for a young gentlewoman not to speak with unknown gentlemen, but a proper 'thank you' surely is in order," said he, still holding one of the books she had dropped.

Elizabeth had been in a sour mood all morning, what with her aunt's insistence she wear that ridiculous pink garb with the flouncy bottom. It was certainly not one that Elizabeth would have chosen for herself, for she much preferred muslin over silk for such an occasion. Then, too, her aunt had insisted that Elizabeth take the carriage to the village when it was a perfectly fine day for a walk. The gentleman's superior attitude only increased her ire.

"Sir, if you had been paying attention to where you were going, then our near collision would have been avoided in its entirety."

He bowed ever so slightly. "Your point is well taken." He turned over the book in his hand and silently read the title. It was but one of several books she had procured to familiarise herself with horse racing. He arched his brow. "My, what interesting taste in books you have, young lady."

His tone dripping with sarcasm did nothing to recommend him. Before she could fashion a retort, Betsy bounced from around the corner. "Miss Eliza—" As if remembering her place, she coloured and corrected her manner of speaking. "Miss Bennet, I beg your pardon for not coming to your aid sooner."

"Miss Elizabeth Bennet." An amused looked played across his face. "Your burden is heavy. May I assist you and see you to your carriage?"

Elizabeth handed her armload over to Betsy. She extended her gloved hand to the stranger, silently beckoning him to surrender her book. "No, sir, it is entirely unnecessary." He still did not relinquish the book—the last relic between them. She arched her brow.

Eventually he looked down, and he must have recalled that he was indeed holding something that belonged to her. He handed it over. "Enjoy your reading, Miss Elizabeth Bennet."

"I have every intention of doing just that, sir, and I would ask you to pay attention to where you are walking."

Elizabeth and her companion walked away, and she had the satisfaction of believing that she had prickled the haughty stranger's swollen pride if only a little. By his manner of dress, his manner of speech, and his proud mien, he was a nobleman—perhaps even a Duke. *I wager he is not accustomed to women who do not bow at his feet.*

"Arrogant, pompous man," Elizabeth said in a low voice intended for her own gratification.

Betsy gaped. "Miss Elizabeth, are you not aware with whom you were speaking just then?"

Elizabeth shrugged. Whomever he was made no difference to her. "No—I have no idea."

"Why, that was Mr. Darcy of Pemberley and Derbyshire."

There was no hiding the curiosity in Lady Vanessa's eyes when Elizabeth returned from her solitary ramble. "Elizabeth, my dear, Betsy tells me that you had the privilege of making Mr. Darcy's acquaintance earlier today."

Taking a seat opposite her ladyship, Elizabeth furrowed her brow. *I do not know that I would deem it a privilege.*

"You must tell me all about him, for I have yet to make his acquaintance. Mr. Darcy, you see, is a recent addition to our society. He is renowned as being the proud owner of some of the finest thoroughbreds in all of England. You must tell me what you think of him." Her ladyship paused a moment but not nearly long enough for Elizabeth to fashion a response.

"I am somewhat acquainted with his Fitzwilliam relatives, Lord and Lady Matlock, and I met his parents, the late Mr. Darcy and the late Lady Anne Darcy as well. He hails from Derbyshire, and he is the young master of Pemberley, one of the finest estates in the county. I know little else of him. Pray, is he amiable? Is he a handsome man?"

"Though our meeting was by happenstance, as Betsy likely told you, I do not know that I would describe him as amiable." *In fact, I found him arrogant and a bit condescending.* "As for your second question on whether he is handsome, I would say he is tolerable." *Yes—tolerable is the word I would choose.*

"Tolerable? Your description of the gentleman is in striking contrast to how Betsy described him. She spoke of his tall person and handsome mien and his eyes. She said if one were not careful, one might risk drowning in his eyes."

Clenching her hands, Elizabeth drew a deep breath. "Your ladyship, you asked me for my opinion. If you find Betsy's opinion more to your liking, then you need not have bothered soliciting mine."

"In such a case as this, I shall rely on my own opinion. He has been a bit of a recluse since his arrival, but that will change soon enough. I suspect we shall both see the gentleman tomorrow. He is staying at Avondale with his friend Lord Andrew Holland, the future Earl of Bosley. Lord Holland shall make the introductions, and then I will know what to think." With a gleam in her eyes, Lady Vanessa leaned closer to her niece. "You shall appreciate Lord Holland. Indeed, he is handsome and amiable, and there can be no differing opinions on the matter. What is more, he has yet to choose a bride. I fear none of the simpering young ladies of the *ton* suit him. I am most anxious for you to make the viscount's acquaintance."

"You speak of the viscount with such fondness, Lady Vanessa."

"Indeed, and there is a good reason. His mother is Lady Clarissa Holland. She and my late husband were siblings. I adore her. She is my closest friend, and we rely upon each other."

Lady Vanessa expounded upon their history: how Lady Clarissa had secured her future by marrying the rich and powerful Lord Lawrence Holland, thus making it possible for Sir Frederick Barrett to bequeath his entire fortune to Lady Vanessa. In their thirty years of marriage, Lord and Lady Holland had only one child, Lord Andrew. For Lady Clarissa's part, she doted on her son exceedingly.

Her ladyship's voice filled with longing. "Since my dear Frederick departed this earth, I feel the pain of our having no children—someone to carry on his legacy. I suppose the reason

I am so very fond of young Holland is because he is the last male of the Barrett lineage. Oh, but his fortune shall be great once he ascends to the earldom—which cannot be soon enough, if you ask me. However, none of that is any of my concern. Although he will not benefit from the Barrett family fortune directly, perhaps his children and their children will benefit from it yet."

Vanity and Pride

Whatever a beautiful spring day it turned out to be. Just as Lady Vanessa had foretold, the landed gentry, along with their families, travelled from miles away to enjoy the day's racing contests. The finale was a high-stakes challenge between two gentlemen who prided themselves as owners of the fastest bays in the county, one being Mr. Fitzwilliam Darcy, and the other being Sir Robert Scott. The event was meant to put an end to speculations once and for all.

Although Elizabeth enjoyed the contest, she could not boast of having any particular interest in the outcome. The same could not be said of the rest of the spectators. The close finish provided the means of a spirited debate amongst Lady Vanessa and her immediate circle. In her haste to put as much distance between Lady Vanessa and her society friends, who were too much like her ladyship for Elizabeth's comfort, and seize a moment of quiet solitude while she could, Elizabeth walked right past Mr. Darcy without acknowledging him.

"Miss Bennet."

She cringed. *Heavens, pray he does not think I came this way for the purpose of putting myself in his path.* She halted her steps, turned about, and faced him. "Mr. Darcy."

"May I have a word with you?"

Despite her aunt's glowing commendations, Elizabeth proceeded cautiously, still annoyed by the manner of her initial acquaintance with the gentleman and what she supposed was mocking on his part, especially now as she recalled his derisive manner when he spoke of her choice of reading material.

She walked to where he stood and curtsied. "Congratulations, Mr. Darcy."

He bowed slightly. "I thank you, according to the common mode of discourse in such situations as this. However, I take no credit other than that of the proud owner of one of the finest bays in the land."

Elizabeth regarded him with an arched smile. "How very like you, sir. The perfect amount of humility cloaked in haughtiness."

A tall, handsome gentleman, blessed with long dark hair and amazing dark eyes, joined them. Having overheard Elizabeth's retort, he playfully slapped Darcy on his back. "That is my friend Darcy, to be sure." He turned to Darcy. "Am I to be introduced?"

Mr. Darcy nodded in acquiescence. "Miss Bennet, allow me to introduce Lord Andrew Holland, future Earl of Bosley. This is Miss Bennet, my lord. She hails from—" His voice trailed off as he looked expectantly at Elizabeth.

"Hertfordshire, my lord," she said, proffering her hand.

He took Elizabeth's hand and raised it to his lips. "It is a pleasure to make your acquaintance."

Elizabeth's eyes filled with mirth. "The pleasure is all mine."

Darcy directed his attention to his approaching groom and then stepped away to confer with him while Elizabeth and Lord Holland continued speaking.

"My aunt will be very disappointed to learn that I have made your acquaintance, my lord, for she speaks very highly of you. She wished to have the honour of introducing us."

His blank expression urged Elizabeth on. "Lady Vanessa Barrett."

Recognition graced his countenance. "Lady Barrett is my aunt as well. Her late husband and my mother were brother and sister." He swept his eyes over Elizabeth. "So you are the young woman of whom Lady Vanessa has spoken so highly. You will forgive me for not realising the connection sooner, I pray. I agree. She will be disappointed, and she is not one who brokers disappointment well. Perhaps we might pretend this meeting never took place, and then her hopes will not have suffered."

"How very thoughtful of you to recommend we deceive her ladyship under the guise of appeasing her, my lord."

The dashing viscount clutched his hand over his heart. "I am wounded, Miss Bennet."

Darcy resumed his place by his friend's side and placed his hand on Lord Holland's shoulder. "Fear not, my friend, for whatever charge Miss Bennet has levelled upon you merely was intended to divert you. I have a strong suspicion that the young lady finds great enjoyment in professing opinions that, in fact, are not her own, solely for sport."

Elizabeth laughed heartily at this picture of herself. "Now, it is my turn to be wounded. Mr. Darcy has attempted to sketch my character in a manner that would have one believe I am harsh and unfeeling when nothing can be further from the truth, and here in a part of the world where so little is known about me that I hoped to pass myself off with some degree of credit."

Darcy smiled and said, "On the contrary, Miss Bennet. I, for one, find your manner entirely refreshing, and I find your taste in books equally so."

A bubbly young woman approached them, rounding out their party. Judging by the young lady's decidedly unguarded manner, Elizabeth could only suppose she was an intimate acquaintance of the viscount's. She swatted him with her fan. "Lord Holland, you will forgive me, but I am most anxious for the pleasure of your company." He accepted her proffered hand and brushed his lips across her knuckles.

"Miss Lancaster, it is always a pleasure to see you. Have you met my friends?"

Her demeanour told him she had not. "Then might I have the honour? First, allow me to introduce you to Mr. Darcy of Pemberley and Derbyshire. Darcy, Miss Lancaster." Darcy bowed and she curtsied. "Secondly, meet Miss Bennet of Hertfordshire."

The ladies greeted each other cordially. Miss Lancaster was no more than one or two and twenty; her face was pretty, her figure tall and striking, and her manner graceful. "Must we be so formal, Miss Bennet? You may call me Miss Lucy or Lucy if you truly prefer to part with the formalities. What might I call you?"

"My given name is Elizabeth Bennet."

"So, you hail from Hertfordshire, do you?" She touched her hand to her head. "Are you Lady Vanessa's niece? Well of course you are! Her ladyship has spoken to my mother of very little since she learned you would be coming for a visit." She outstretched her arms. "Welcome to Bosley." Closing them, she placed her hand on Elizabeth's arm. "Now we absolutely must dispense with the formalities, for we shall spend a great deal of time with each other in the coming months."

"I shall look forward to it."

The gregarious young woman then laced her hand through Lord Holland's crossed arms. "Indeed. Please pardon me for a moment. I need a moment with this fine gentleman."

Once again, Elizabeth found herself alone with Mr. Darcy. *Why is he merely staring at me?* Elizabeth looked at him expect-

antly; after all, he had been the one to summon her to his side.
"If I may ask, what is the purpose of my standing here, sir?"

"Pardon?"

"Earlier, you said you wanted to speak with me. I am listening."

"I simply wanted to—" He paused for a moment. Moistening his lips, his gaze pored over Elizabeth. "I supposed I wanted to speak with you—"

"Then, I suppose that whatever it was you wanted to say to me has since slipped your mind."

"You might say that."

What an exasperating man! When Miss Lancaster spoke of us spending time in company, I wonder if that includes spending time with him. He is Lord Holland's house guest, and I imagine Miss Lancaster does not often forego the chance to be in his lordship's company. Elizabeth's thoughts wandered back to her current companion. If she were to judge by the manner in which he looked at her, she would swear he was looking for a flaw in her appearance—perhaps some failure of perfect symmetry in her form. Elizabeth's courage always rose in the face of any such attempts to intimidate her. As with her aunt, she intended for Mr. Darcy to know it. She arched her brow. "Senility—I pray that is not a family trait, Mr. Darcy."

Before the gentleman could fashion a retort, a passerby interrupted them with congratulations on Mr. Darcy's victory. Elizabeth glanced to where Lord Holland and Miss Lancaster stood. *By the look of things, Miss Lancaster would like very much to be the future mistress of Avondale. I must admit they are a striking pair.*

The couple's return put an end to Elizabeth's musings. Lord Holland stood next to his friend. "Well, Darcy, it seems that we are obliged to attend a picnic tomorrow."

A bemused expression crossed Mr. Darcy's face. "A picnic?"

Lord Holland smiled fondly at the young woman attached to his arm. "The lady insists."

"Well, you did promise me that you would have a picnic at Avondale, did you not. I prognosticate that tomorrow will be such a fine day. I am sure Mr. Darcy will find the occasion diverting. You must be sure to invite Miss Elizabeth."

The viscount gazed at Elizabeth. "What say you to a picnic, Miss Bennet?"

Glad for the opportunity to spend time with people her own age, Elizabeth was inclined to accept immediately. However, these people were strangers. Some measure of prudence was warranted. "As I only just met you, your lordship, may I presume to ask who else will be in attendance?"

Lucy said, "Why, solely the four of us. Lord Holland will not take no for an answer, will you, my lord?"

The viscount said nothing, which was all the encouragement Miss Lancaster needed. "There, you see. The four of us shall have a picnic at Avondale tomorrow. What a lovely time it shall be!"

Elizabeth could hardly wait to commit the events of the day to paper when she returned to Barrington Hall that evening after having dined at Avondale along with her aunt and several other prominent guests in celebration of Mr. Darcy's victory. As the winning bay was a thoroughbred he had recently acquired from Lord Holland's father and the winning purse was upwards of one hundred pounds, it was indeed a cause for celebration for the House of Avondale as well.

Her mind filled with the perplexing man, Elizabeth took her place at her writing desk and began.

> The tall, distinguished gentleman I met in the village a few days prior is Mr. Darcy. It turns out he is not a peer after all, but he might as well be. By Lady Vanessa's account, he descends from a long line of aristocrats. I have even learned he has ten thousand pounds a year, and he is the young master of one of the finest estates in Derbyshire. Though it matters not in the least to me, the gentleman is single. Just think what Mama would say! What I say is that he is haugh-

ty and condescending, and he likely thinks very highly of himself. The only reason I bother to write about him at all is because I had the 'pleasure' of spending such a great stretch of time in his company today. Never have I felt myself to be so closely observed than I did when with him. He is a man of sense and education, and were I to be completely honest, I would have to confess that his Adonis-like features render him exceedingly agreeable to look at. I suppose he has the capacity to be charming should he wish it, but I shall reserve judgement for now. I shall see how he behaves tomorrow.

I also had the pleasure of meeting Lady Vanessa's nephew, today—Lord Andrew Holland. Oh, what a handsome man he is with his tall person, his dark eyes, and his perfect, dark hair. I am rather certain I was not the only member of our party who regarded him so, for I also had the privilege of meeting a Miss Lucy Lancaster. What a charming creature she is. I think we shall get along swimmingly.

Chapter 4

For Having Suffered

The foursome never did have a picnic that next day. Prior to
the planned outing, Lord Holland treated his guests to an
exhibition of his horsemanship prowess. Darcy, Elizabeth, and
Lucy watched his lordship execute the row of hurdles with the
adroitness of a seasoned jockey. One by one, he accomplished
each feat without incident, and then it happened. His horse
failed to clear the last hurdle on the course. Lord Holland went
flying through the air. Horrified by what they saw, the spectators, which included members of his staff, raced to the field.

Elizabeth gasped at the horrific sight. The viscount lay
stretched out on the ground, motionless, his head swimming in
a crimson pool of blood. Shouting orders to a servant to summon the physician, Darcy and the attending groom acted
quickly to remove the viscount to the manor house.

The entire household was in turmoil over the fate of the future earl. Lady Vanessa had been summoned to attend Lady Clarissa. Consoling the panic-stricken mother proved difficult. Her wailing flooded the halls. After spending several hours with the viscount, the physician, whose bloodstained clothing bore evidence of Lord Holland's suffering, descended the stairs with the prognosis. Lord Holland had lost a significant amount of blood and remained unconscious. His words set off a cascade of disheartening refrains: we must wait and see and pray for the best.

We must wait and see and pray for the best. Those ten little words struck Elizabeth like a bolt of lightning. There had been only one other time in her life that she heard those words, and that had proved to be the most heartrending day of her life. *We must wait and see and pray for the best.*

Elizabeth drifted towards the window, her heart heavy with grief and her eyes leaden with unshed tears. It was too much. The pain she believed she had taught herself to endure with quiet grace and dignity threatened to flood her entire being. Unwilling to allow anyone to bear witness to the depths of her despair, she raced from the room.

Darcy had watched in wonder as Elizabeth paced the floor the entire time that the physician was with his friend. As disquieted as he had been by the physician's prognosis, Elizabeth's reaction struck him as particularly troubling. *Given her brief acquaintance with his lordship, how can she possibly be so distressed by any of this? Surely she had been traumatised by the sight of the viscount lying on the ground, his head swimming in blood.* Who was to say how long a gently bred young woman would carry such an image around with her. However, even Miss Lancaster, whom Darcy knew to be quite taken with Lord Holland, did not wear her anguish as openly as did Miss Elizabeth. *No—something greater is at the root of her discomfort.*

When Elizabeth bolted from the room, Darcy was not long in following her. He walked fast to catch up with her. Once she became aware of his presence, she halted her frantic pace and allowed him to accompany her. He longed to reach for her, to take her in his arms, and to comfort her. He clasped his hands behind his back to stop himself.

"Thou doth not see," Mr. Darcy said, his voice tender and soothing. "Neither intruder, nor foe, nor stranger unknown. Thou shalt not fear—for thou are not alone."

Elizabeth gazed up at his face. "I am not familiar with that particular stanza, sir."

"It is personal, from me to you."

Elizabeth studied his eyes and saw in them something she had never seen before—compassion.

"Lord Holland is young and vibrant; he shall recover."

"I know you are correct, sir."

"I cannot help but feel you are disturbed by concerns of a different matter. It might help to talk about what is truly at the root of your worries."

"I recall the last time I was with someone whose prognosis was the same as Lord Holland's physician described. She never recovered."

"She?"

"My sister ... Jane."

"I am sorry."

She reached for the brooch she always kept close to her heart—an exquisitely carved ornament, which contained a lock of Elizabeth's beloved sister's golden hair encased on one side and her sister's likeness on the other. Opening it, she showed it to Darcy. "This is Jane."

"Your sister was beautiful ... and so young."

Elizabeth nodded in acknowledgement. "Jane was always considered the beauty in the family. She was kind and good and always saw the best in everyone. Never had she uttered an unkind word."

"Is your loss recent?"

"Nearly two years have passed." Elizabeth closed her brooch, and her eyes drifted towards the sun settling over the horizon. "I should have done more. My sister needed me, and I failed her."

Darcy placed his hand on Elizabeth's arm. "Would you like to talk about what happened?"

Caught between despair over what she had seen earlier and longing to share her sorrow with another living being, she hardly recognised her own voice. "My papa did not want me to be there. He feared I was too young, but what he failed to understand was there was no place else on earth for me. I would have traded places with my sister if I could have." Her eyes prickled with tears. "Jane died in my arms."

There had been a succession of rainy days from the moment her beloved sister fell ill until the day she found peace. Melancholy had become Elizabeth's favourite companion whenever rain poured from the skies. The unspoken truth was that the incident needed not to have happened. Elizabeth's mother had the idea of sending Jane to a neighbouring estate nearly five miles from Longbourn on horseback in a misguided attempt to land a husband. Halfway into the journey, common sense had prevailed, and Jane returned home, but not soon enough to escape the onset of what Mrs. Bennet had proclaimed a trifling cold. Whether or not Mrs. Bennet suffered any guilt as a result of the tragedy was hard to say, but things had never been the same at Longbourn ever since that time. Elizabeth wanted to find fault in someone, but to ascribe blame to her mother was not something she would allow, even as a passing thought. Hence, she took the burden upon herself.

Darcy wanted nothing more than to touch Elizabeth's face and wipe away her tears, but he could not. Such a show of affection surely exceeded all bounds of decorum. He cupped her hand in his. "You did not fail your sister."

Elizabeth looked deep into his eyes and then slowly pulled away her hand. *What am I doing confiding in this man? I hardly know him.* Sniffing her tears, she managed a slight smile. "Of course you are correct, sir. As time goes on, I realise there is little I could have done. But then a dreadful accident like this occurs, and I find myself experiencing the harrowing pain of losing my sister all over again."

Recalling how hopeless she felt during Jane's ordeal, Elizabeth resolved that she must do something, anything to set her mind upon a different course. "There is an urgent matter that I must attend."

"What is it?"

"You will see." She led him into the rose garden. "Sir, may I borrow your pocket knife?"

"My knife?"

She arched her brow. "You do possess one, do you not?"

"I do, but what are you planning to do with a knife?"

"What do you think I plan to do?" She stepped closer and held out her hand. "I shall gather a fresh bouquet of flowers and send them to Lord Holland."

"There is a fine idea. Perhaps the aroma will revive him."

"Do not make light of my scheme unless you have a better idea, Mr. Darcy."

"I was thinking of giving him a good shake for his perilous attempts to impress you, followed by a stern speech. His lordship hates any sort of rebuke. He will want to put forth a proper rebuttal."

"What say you we first try my way?"

Later that evening, Elizabeth paced the floor. In spite of the lateness of the hour, sleep was the furthest thing from her mind. She had stayed at Avondale for as long as decorum allowed and finally accepted an offer of the Holland carriage to return her to Barrington Hall. Lady Vanessa spent the night at Avondale with a mind of being of some service to Lady Clarissa. Events of the day wreaked havoc in Elizabeth's composure, and she knew but one way to calm herself.

I have not felt as awful as I did today for a very long time—not since the day I lost you. It was painful to suffer many of those same feelings again. I pray for a happier outcome than my fears portend—that I shall soon receive word that Lord Holland has awakened. The alternative is untenable for his friends and his acquaintances and especially for his mother, Lady Clarissa. She was most inconsolable today. She is most fortunate to have such a dear friend in Lady Vanessa who remains by her side.

I, too, found a comforting presence in the form of Mr. Darcy. Until today, I truly suspected the gentleman barely tolerated me, and his wont of looking at me was merely to find fault. Today, I witnessed a different side of him: a kind, gentle, and attentive being. He allowed—nay, encouraged me to show my pain by being an unbiased listener and a reassuring voice of reason. If it is possible for men and women to be friends, then I believe I have found a friend in Mr. Darcy.

Chapter 5

The Trouble of Liking Them

Darcy stared out the window and into the emptiness that preceded dawn's awakening. The sound of his friend stirring in bed beckoned his attention. He whispered a silent prayer in thanks and proceeded to Lord Holland's bedside. He pulled up a chair. "You gave us quite a scare, my friend."

His lordship glanced over and peered at the darkness outside. "What time is it?" He reached his hand to his head and felt the bandage. "What happened?"

"Do you not recall? You were making a spectacle of yourself for the young ladies, and your horse took a tumble."

Lord Holland attempted to sit up, but Darcy silently urged him to remain settled. "Pegasus took a tumble? Is ... is he—?"

"Fear not. Your darling Pegasus met with no harm. However, according to your physician, you suffered a severe blow to the head. You have been unconscious for hours."

"Miss Bennet—what must she be thinking?"

As grateful as Darcy was to have his friend awake, hearing Elizabeth's name amongst the first words the viscount uttered unsettled him. *How strange that he would worry over Miss Elizabeth's reaction when Miss Lancaster was also present when the accident occurred. He has known her for years. By all indications, she is quite taken with him, whereas he only made Miss Elizabeth's acquaintance days prior.*

"Both Miss Bennet and Miss Lancaster were finally persuaded to return to their own homes after waiting here for hours. I shall make certain they receive word of your recovery at morning's first light. I fear it is too early to disturb them now, but I will summon the physician and let him know you are awake."

Lord Holland stirred once again. "I will not have anyone make a fuss over me."

Darcy held out his hand to still his friend. "If you had been privy to the spectacle of it all, I daresay you would not speak this way. Do you suppose I would be here as opposed to the comforts of my own bed were your situation not tenuous?"

"Have you been here the entire time?"

"For the most part, I was here, as well as your mother and Lady Barrett."

"I suppose the flowers are my mother's doing?"

"On the contrary, the flowers were cut fresh and arranged by another."

"Who other than my mother would even think to bring me flowers? Is this Lucy's doing?"

"Actually, it was Miss Bennet."

Lord Holland smiled, and then he winced in pain. "That was quite considerate of her."

"Indeed. Miss Bennet was beside herself with worry, having suffered a painfully similar situation herself."

"I shall look forward to seeing her and thank her properly."

"Seeing you up and about will be the best way to accomplish that. Now do as you are told. Lie here and wait while I summon the physician."

It took nearly a fortnight, but the bandages were finally re-moved for the last time, signalling the viscount's recovery from his fall. His recuperation was well timed, for he was to welcome additional house guests at Avondale—the Bingleys.

His smile wavering, the younger gentleman said, "You must forgive me. I know your invitation was meant solely for me, but my sister Caroline insisted. You know I cannot deny her any-thing. Believe me, I have tried."

Lord Holland understood his friend Charles Bingley's easy-going temperament and his friend's sister's fierce determina-tion well enough to comprehend completely the younger man. "Do not concern yourself. It is no imposition. We have ample room, and I am certain my mother will not mind one bit. You know how much she loves to entertain." *And I shall be enter-tained as well, watching Darcy fend off Miss Bingley's impassioned pursuit.*

"I knew you would understand. I pray Darcy will be as amiable."

Darcy sauntered into the room in time to catch Bingley's last words. "When have you ever known me to be less than amiable, Charles?"

Bingley's face lit up at the sight of his closest friend and mentor. "Heavens, Darcy, I do not know a more awful object than you at your own house especially, and of a Sunday evening when you have nothing to do."

Silently acknowledging Bingley's point was well taken, the two men shook hands. "It is nice to see you, old friend."

"Yes, but as I was just saying, you may not be equally de-lighted when you discover who else has joined us."

Darcy's face contorted into a tight grimace. Charles shrugged. "I am sorry, old fellow, but she insisted." He shook his head. "You know how she is when her mind is fixed upon a matter. There is simply no saying 'no' to her."

Later that evening, when she and Lady Vanessa arrived at Avondale, Elizabeth was met with a most unwelcomed surprise. While she knew it was to be a large gathering where she was likely to form new acquaintances, she hardly expected this.

What on earth is she doing here? Elizabeth could well imagine the object of her silent inquiry asking herself the same question. When the two had met in Hertfordshire under a year ago, they had not been the best of friends despite their being neighbours. Miss Caroline Bingley and her sister, Mrs. Louisa Hurst, had suffered their time at Netherfield Park, their brother's newly acquired estate, as though it were a sentencing of the direst kind.

Elizabeth bit her lip to hide her amusement in recollecting her neighbours' antics. Although always impeccably dressed in the latest fashions, Caroline's penchant for burnt-orange gowns and flouncy feathers made her stand out in that evening's gathering of high-society people just as she did amidst the rather limited society of Hertfordshire. Elizabeth quickly glanced about the room. *I wonder why Mrs. Hurst is not hovering nearby.* The two superior sisters were inseparable—inseparable, haughty, and particularly condescending—when Elizabeth first made their acquaintance. *One would never know their family's fortune was earned in trade—a fact that must surely have escaped their own knowing judging by the deplorable manner in which they disdain anyone whom they deemed beneath them.* Elizabeth resisted a smirk. *I wonder what my aunt will think of those two.*

The reservations Elizabeth suffered over the prospect of spending an entire evening with the Bingley sisters were erased when she espied the amiable Charles Bingley standing off to the side of the room. Upon seeing her, he made his way to Elizabeth's side, and with a gregarious and handsome smile, he reminded Elizabeth why she had always found it a pleasure being in his company.

What a stir his coming to the neighbourhood and letting Netherfield Park had incited amongst all the mammas with unwed daughters, proclaiming a single man with a good fortune must be in want of a wife. With the task of marrying so many daughters resting squarely on her shoulders, Mrs. Bennet was especially eager to see one of them as the mistress of the fine estate. As much as she liked Mr. Bingley, Elizabeth could never engender anything beyond sisterly affection towards him. She rather supposed her sentiments had more to do with her sister Jane than anything. *He is just the sort of gentleman Jane would have adored.*

Elizabeth's younger sisters could not be prevailed upon to pay attention to Mr. Bingley either, what with Mary's wont of citing Fordyce's sermons and other moral platitudes when it came to such matters, and Kitty and Lydia's ceaseless regard for any man in a uniform. But her dearest Jane—a match between Jane and Bingley might have been perfect. Elizabeth could imagine her sister proclaiming him everything a gentleman ought to be. *For Jane, there was no greater commendation.*

Elizabeth quietly sighed. She was finally reaching a point where her memories of her beloved sister no longer rekindled the throbbing ache in her heart. For that she was exceedingly grateful. *Jane would want me to be at peace.*

Mr. Bingley cleared his throat. "Miss Bennet, it is such a delight seeing you here. How are you?"

Elizabeth curtsied and assured him that all was well.

He conversed in a friendly, though general way, and looked and spoke with the same good-humoured ease that he had ever done. "How is your family? Your sisters? Did any of them travel with you?"

"All of my sisters remain in Hertfordshire. I am staying with my aunt, Lady Vanessa Barrett."

"Then I shall be delighted to make her acquaintance."

"And your sisters—did both of them travel with you?"

"My eldest sister remains in London."

At least having to bother with only one of them was a cause for celebration. *Unfortunately, it is the worst one of them.*

Miss Caroline Bingley approached them, but by the put-off expression on her face, Elizabeth surmised it was the last thing she wanted to do. Charles said, "Caroline, look who it is—our neighbour from Hertfordshire."

A pinched expression marred Caroline's face. "Miss Eliza Bennet, what a surprise this is."

"Miss Bingley, I would have to say the same."

Bingley bestowed a good-hearted smile. "Not an unwelcome surprise, I assure you. I could not be more pleased." He turned to his sister. "Miss Bennet is in Bosley visiting her relation, a Lady Vanessa Barrett. I was just saying that I look forward to making her acquaintance during our brief stay."

"Lady Vanessa Barrett?" Caroline's countenance smacked of shock and genuine horror.

"Yes, she is my father's sister."

"Why, I rather supposed all your relatives were on your mother's side of the family."

"I do not comprehend why you would have supposed such a thing. Surely you recall making the acquaintance of my cousin Mr. Collins."

Caroline scowled. "But of course." The bored expression on her face quickly went from disaffected disgust to enraptured anticipation. Elizabeth followed the path of Caroline's eyes to ascertain what had brought about such a change.

Elizabeth's own eyes opened wide when she saw the object of Caroline's unmasked esteem was Mr. Darcy. *Does the lady know the gentleman, or is she simply taken by his tall person, his broad shoulders, his well-crafted legs, his alluring eyes—* Elizabeth caught herself. When had she begun to see him as such?

Caroline seized hold of her brother's arm. "Come, Charles. We must speak with Mr. Darcy."

"I will do no such thing. I am speaking with Miss Bennet

just now," he said, shaking his arm free.

"But if you do not go and speak to him, then I cannot go."

"When has that ever stopped you before, Caroline? Besides, I have already spoken with Darcy."

The siblings continued their banter as if Elizabeth were not standing there and hearing every word of the awkward exchange. Elizabeth pretended she was much caught up with everything else taking place in the room, and all the while she thought of how little had changed between the two of them.

"How could you have spoken to him when this is the first I have seen of him since our arrival? Oh, Charles, I insist that you escort me across the room so Mr. Darcy will be aware of my presence."

"He knows you are here."

"Oh! He does? Did he ask after me? What did he say?"

Charles looked at Elizabeth apologetically.

"Please, Mr. Bingley, do not let me detain you. I shall be delighted to speak with you over the course of the evening."

Before Charles could fashion a reply, his sister was leading him across the room in Darcy's direction. He must have seen them coming, but for a reason Elizabeth could not discern, the gentleman turned on his heels and headed in the opposite direction.

Later, when the gentlemen joined the ladies in the drawing room after dinner, Elizabeth sat off in a quiet corner and observed Mr. Darcy's tortured countenance while standing with Mr. Bingley's sister. *Mr. Darcy has shown himself to be someone I can trust with my most heartfelt secrets. The least I might do is intercede on his behalf and spare him an evening of torment from the likes of Caroline Bingley.*

In a manner reminiscent of her friend Lucy's wont of commanding Lord Holland's undivided attention, Elizabeth walked to where Mr. Darcy and Caroline stood and laced her arm through his. "Mr. Darcy, you promised to turn the pages for me when it was my turn to exhibit this evening. Shall we proceed to the pianoforte?"

For the first time that evening, she observed his warm smile. It was enough to take her breath away.

With his other hand, Darcy brushed his thumb atop the back of her hand resting on his arm. "Indeed, Miss Bennet. Pardon me, Miss Bingley." It was next to impossible for Elizabeth not to glance over her shoulder to gauge the other woman's reaction as they were walking away. Apparently rendered speechless, the colour in Caroline's face rivalled the hue of her gown.

When they were comfortably seated, Elizabeth commenced poring through the music sheets while Darcy said, "How can I thank you?"

"It was nothing, sir. I saw what must be done, and I did it."

"You were very astute in coming to my service. I take it you know the Bingleys."

"Yes, I made their acquaintance in Hertfordshire."

"Ah, yes. I recall Bingley writing to tell me he had let an estate in Hertfordshire."

"Indeed—Netherfield Park. Miss Bingley made quite an impression on everyone."

"Please, I would much rather we discuss anything except Miss Caroline Bingley."

"Then what shall we talk about, Mr. Darcy? We must have some conversation."

"I would rather we speak on any number of subjects so long as there is no mention of Bingley's sister. Perhaps we might discuss books, music, or even the weather."

"I take it the lady is not one of your favourite people."

"Indeed, your coming to my rescue was a godsend. You saved me from a torturous situation." His smile spoke to his gratitude. Leaning in closer to Elizabeth, he said, "I owe you, and I insist upon paying my debt."

There was but one thing Elizabeth wanted more than anything from Mr. Darcy, but did she dare ask it of this rich and powerful man? Biting her lip, she pondered how best to proceed. Hints of reservation crept into her voice. "In that case, I know what I would like."

"What is it?"

"You will think I am being presumptuous—"

"Ask me anything. I am in your power."

She ceased what she was doing and looked him straight in the eyes. "Teach me to ride horseback."

He answered yes!

Elizabeth could almost feel the icy stares that came her way as she and Mr. Darcy continued their amiable discourse. Miss Bingley was more than a little dissatisfied by the events unfolding at the pianoforte. She was not the only one suffering displeasure. Lord Holland was vexed as well.

Despite arriving home late from Avondale, Elizabeth could not rest until she had captured the events of the evening on paper. Sitting at the desk in her dimly lighted room, she began.

> Never once did I imagine myself crossing paths with Caroline Bingley here in Bosley. What I had supposed was disdain and condescension towards the people in Meryton is merely her way, for she displays that same annoyingly superior attitude here—at least towards me. Towards Mr. Darcy, she is another woman. I believe she holds the gentleman in the highest esteem. It is most unfortunate that he does not return her regard. On more than one occasion, I saw him quit the room altogether to avoid her. I never thought I would say this, but I will say it just the same: poor Caroline. I did not help matters. When she finally managed to secure him all to herself, after an evening of cat and mouse, where she was the former and he the latter, I interceded on Mr. Darcy's behalf and stole him away from her. Now Caroline has even more reason to think poorly of me—something I supposed was impossible when last I saw of her in Hertfordshire.

It seems my sacrifice is to be handsomely rewarded, for Mr. Darcy has agreed to teach me to ride horseback. I know I always said that I shall never have a need to learn how to ride, preferring to enjoy the comfort of a carriage when walking is not an option, but I have been thinking about changing my stance for quite some time. Lucy and Lord Holland are particularly fond of riding, and they have suggested we do so on many occasions. As we are to be a foursome, it is only fitting that I learn to ride, and who better to teach me than the 'master' as I have no doubt he would proclaim himself. Still, I was exceedingly surprised he agreed to my request to teach me, for in asking such a favour, I had intended to be impertinent. The gentleman is full of surprises. Now I have but one question: what will Caroline do once she finds out?

Chapter 6

Without Being Vain

The next day, Darcy and Elizabeth sat together on a blanket spread underneath a giant oak, both satisfied with the morning's lesson. Elizabeth smoothed her riding habit skirt. Betsy had it laid out on the bed when Elizabeth completed her morning toilette. She had never owned such a fine outfit. How Betsy knew she needed it on that particular morning was a mystery.

More than once, her companion had robbed her of her composure during the riding lesson: innocent brushes of his hands against hers, gentle caresses as he assisted her in mounting and dismounting the horse, the melodic sound of his voice as he gave her instructions, and the warmth of his breath against her skin when he leaned in closer than likely was warranted to gently remind her of a particular technique that had slipped her mind. How she had managed to keep track of a single thing was a wonder.

Even now, her entire body was all too aware of his nearness. Rather than ponder too long the reason he made her feel this way, she endeavoured to break their silence with a dose of light-heartedness. "I never supposed you would bring your own horse, Mr. Darcy. Then again, perhaps my aunt's horses do not suit."

"This is no ordinary horse."

"Heaven forbid! No one would dare accuse the owner of some of the finest bays in the country of possessing an *ordinary* horse."

"I suppose my reputation in that regard precedes me. Or has your reading about the history of horse racing led you to the discovery of an edition of *The Jockey's Book*?"

"I am afraid I have barely started my book on the history of horse racing. By the bye, I have not quite forgiven you for your teasing manner when we first met."

"I was not teasing. I was merely intrigued. It is not often that I meet someone of the fairer sex who shows an interest in an area that is so near and dear to my heart."

"What better way to improve one's mind than through extensive reading?"

"Reading has its purposes, and, indeed, the constant improvement of one's mind is but one of them. However, I much prefer a vigorous horseback ride."

"I am beginning to wonder if there is anything that you prefer to horses, Mr. Darcy."

He smiled. "Well, I can think of one particular pastime that I would opt for over my sport."

"Oh! And what is that?"

Darcy raked his eyes over Elizabeth's body before quickly diverting his gaze. "Perhaps, that is a lesson I will teach you at another time."

Elizabeth's spirits rose to playfulness. "I am not opposed to learning new things, sir. The steady improving of one's mind is essential; however, it would help to know what sort of lesson you have in mind. I find that I am a much better student if I have time to prepare for my lessons in advance."

He took her hand in his. "I would not have you give the matter too much thought, for no advance preparation is required. You will know all you need to know when the time is right, and I suspect it is a subject in which you will triumph."

She leaned in and smiled teasingly. "And this is all the hint I am to receive?"

Darcy released her hand and stood. He reached down and helped Elizabeth to her feet. "I am afraid that is all for today. Come, I will escort you to the house."

When they were at the door, he said, "Miss Bennet, it has been a pleasure spending the morning with you. I shall look forward to our next lesson."

"Will you come inside and enjoy a refreshing drink before returning to Avondale, sir?"

"No—not just now. You shall hear from me again—soon."

Darcy walked away with his head full of Elizabeth. Her face was rendered uncommonly intelligent by the beautiful expression of her dark eyes, and her figure was light and pleasing. Although her manners were not those of the fashionable world, he was caught by their easy playfulness. Darcy had never been so bewitched by any woman as he was by Miss Elizabeth Bennet. He was beginning to feel the danger of paying Elizabeth too much attention, and he was not certain how to feel about that. A man of eight and twenty with a sense of the world, he had every reason to consider that he had it all: rank, privilege, untold wealth, and a strong passion for life and particularly his sport. His love of horse racing was the result of a long-standing tradition that started with his maternal grandfather as well as his father's father. By now, the acquisition of thoroughbred bays was in his blood.

Darcy loved his manner of living, and he was in no hurry to change it.

For her part, Elizabeth marvelled at Mr. Darcy's staggering alteration in attitude. As they walked along in maddening silence, her attempts to further engage him in discourse proved futile in light of his curt replies even to the most open-ended questions. How he had gone from being lively and amiable to brooding and taciturn in a span of a few minutes amazed her. However, there was the promise of another lesson, and that alone was an intriguing prospect.

Upon entering her room, she went straight to her desk. She could not wait to capture all her thoughts on paper.

> I hardly know what to think or how to feel about Mr. Darcy. I want to accuse him of being aloof, but how does that possibly fit with the entirety of his manner during the course of our lesson? He possessed the patience of a saint, for although it was entirely my idea that I should have lessons, the prospect of riding a horse was a bit overwhelming once I found myself so close to the magnificent beast.

> When we were at leisure after our lesson, he spoke of his enjoyment of other pastimes, but he would not say exactly what they were—only a vague promise that he will teach me. My further inquiries did not bode well on his composure, for that is when he grew flustered and ill at ease.

Elizabeth laid her pen aside and gazed out the window. *Whatever am I to make of his change in demeanour?* Some minutes passed in recollection of her day with Mr. Darcy. She released a heavy sigh.

It will not do to think too long on such matters as this. As much as I enjoy Mr. Darcy's company, it would not do to suppose what we share is anything beyond friendship, for I am determined that is all it shall ever be. Knowing as well as I do the pain inherent in the loss of a strong attachment, I mean to protect my heart from any sort of entanglement.

I shall be perfectly content to spend time with Mr. Darcy and enjoy his manner of flattering my ego, for I must confess, he does it very well.

Days later, Lord Holland and Elizabeth rounded the corner of the stable when they espied Darcy and another gentleman. The two were headed their way, deep in conversation. Eager anticipation gripped Elizabeth's body at the sight of Mr. Darcy. It had been a few days since her last riding lesson. Her fervent hope was that he would join them on the tour of the stables. She recognised the other man as the groom who had been with him during the race.

It seemed all he meant to bestow was a curt nod their way, and he was gone directly with the groom in the direction of the yard. Elizabeth was taken aback by Mr. Darcy's behaviour, although she tried unsuccessfully to mask her dismay.

Lord Holland drew her closer by his side. "Is there anything amiss between you and Darcy, Miss Bennet?"

His words gave her to know she was wearing her feelings on her sleeve with regard to Mr. Darcy's slight. *Why else would the viscount ask such a thing unless he sensed it too?*

She drew a quick breath and released it slowly as she pondered what the gentleman was about. Oh, how Mr. Darcy confounded her! "No—not at all. I suppose he is involved in some serious matter as regards one of his *horses*."

"I would say Darcy's primary concern lies with his horses. One must accustom oneself to that fact should they wish to garner his good opinion."

Lord Holland felt it was only fitting that Elizabeth should know and understand the gentleman whom she was allowing to rob her composure. Darcy and he had been acquaintances since their days at Cambridge. When his father, Lord Lawrence Holland, made it known that he was desirous of a healthy infusion of cash and would be willing to go as far as put several of his bays up for sale, Darcy stepped forward to secure the deal.

Darcy and Lord Holland's friendship had grown steadier ever since.

Elizabeth and Lord Holland spent most of the day together. When he escorted her to Barrington Hall, Lady Vanessa insisted he dine with them. Afterwards, her ladyship retired to her apartment early, leaving Elizabeth to entertain their guest. The couple sat in Lady Vanessa's drawing room and talked of many things: the weather, poetry, and their favourite books. There was no topic on which the two could discuss without an equal share of enthusiasm.

"Your interest in books is but one of the things I admire about you, Miss Bennet. If I had to pick my favourite from the list of your estimable qualities, I would have to say the thing I admire most about you is your ability to enjoy the follies of others and laugh at them in their turn, all without giving offence. I hope you never change in that regard."

Puzzled by his speech, Elizabeth arched her brow. "I thank you for the compliment, I think. But why would I ever have cause to change?"

"Pardon me, but your aunt and my mother are very fond of each other. Hence, I am no stranger to the future your aunt has planned for you."

Elizabeth folded her arms over her chest and released a slow steady breath. "I did not think my aunt so indelicate as to discuss such matters with anyone outside our immediate family circle." She valued her privacy. The last thing she wanted was the entire town being privy to her personal concerns, especially if it inspired everyone to think of her as a poor relation who should be beholden to her aunt for her munificence.

"Well, you need not worry. While it is true that my mother is a social butterfly, she is no gossip. She and Lady Vanessa are the dearest of friends." He leaned close to Elizabeth. "Surely you are aware of their grand scheme for *our* future."

Elizabeth shifted a bit and shook her head. "No—I have no idea of any scheme. Perhaps you will enlighten me, my lord."

"Perhaps I have said too much. Their plan shall unfold naturally, and I should hope you will be delighted."

"Pardon me if I speak out of turn, my lord. As best I can tell, Miss Lancaster is very fond of you, and you, no doubt, think highly of her. I have come to consider that *your* futures are aligned."

He dismissively waved his hand. "Then you must put any such notion completely out of your mind. While it is true that Miss Lancaster and I are particularly fond of each other, a factor of our having known each other most of our lives, she is destined for another. In fact, you shall meet him when he returns from the continent."

"Are you quite certain? She has said nothing to me about being engaged."

"I am not surprised. The engagement is of a peculiar sort. She is not entirely reconciled with the match, but it does not signify, for she has no say in the matter. It is arranged, shall we say."

Elizabeth made no attempt to conceal her curiosity. If there existed a chance in the world that she might aid her friend in turning the viscount's head, Elizabeth was determined to pursue it. "How do you feel about her situation?"

"I say it is just as well, for I am in grave danger of losing my heart to another."

"Oh! Have I met her?"

He took her hand and raised it to his lips. "Indeed, you have. I believe you know her well."

It was the night of the Avondale ball, and it being her first since her arrival in Bosley, Elizabeth looked forward to the evening with great excitement. Soon after her arrival, her enthusiasm gave way to perturbation. What had Lord Holland meant by requesting her hand for the opening set? Elizabeth would much rather he had asked Lucy, who was standing next to her and whose mouth gaped over what she surely must have perceived as a slight. As she was not inclined to deny the viscount anything that he deigned to request, Elizabeth threw her friend an apologetic look, accepted his proffered hand, and proceeded to the dance floor.

When those dances were over, she made her way to Lucy's side. Lucy held both hands out in welcome. Elizabeth smiled in gratitude. "Forgive me for dancing with his lordship. I felt I had no choice. You must know that I would rather he had asked you."

"Please, there is no need to apologise. I wager his lordship knows what he is about. He sees me more of a little sister, I fear—as much as I wish otherwise."

"Oh! But you must not surrender all hope in that regard." Elizabeth was about to offer additional words of encouragement to her friend when she found herself suddenly addressed by Mr. Darcy, who, as a consequence of his behaviour of late, took her so much by surprise in his application for her hand that without knowing what she did, she accepted him. He walked away again immediately, and she was left to fret over her own want of presence of mind.

Her friend tried to console her. "I know you are appalled by his slight the other day, but I think you should give him another chance. Surely his asking you for the second set is his way of making amends."

When the dancing recommenced, Darcy approached to claim her hand, and Elizabeth took her place in the set. They stood for some time without speaking a word. She began to imagine that their silence was to last through the two dances, and for her part, she was resolved not to break it. Elizabeth could be equally as taciturn as her dance partner. If they were to speak on any matter at all, then Mr. Darcy would have to be the one to initiate the discourse. He did.

"I am delighted to see you this evening, Miss Bennet."

Elizabeth acknowledged his sentiment and was again silent. After a pause of some minutes, Mr. Darcy addressed her a second time. "You are quiet, Miss Bennet—uncommonly so."

She smiled and assured him that whatever he wished her to say would be said.

"Very well, that reply will do for the present. Perhaps, by and by, I may remark on this dance. I find it quite exhilarating. Now we may be silent."

Silent! She was livid that he had treated her as abominably as he had when last they saw each other, and she could no longer pretend otherwise. "Why did you not speak to me the other day, Mr. Darcy?"

"The other day?"

"Yes, you could not have missed seeing me."

"Well, you were with Lord Holland."

"When has my being with your friend ever been a deterrent?"

"I suppose it was the manner in which the two of you were speaking." They were soon separated by the dance. Once reunited, Darcy said, "You might say I was jealous."

"Jealous? By your manner, you surely fooled me."

"Surely you do not suppose I am incapable of such a sentiment."

"No, I suppose we all have it in us to feel jealous from time to time, although I do not know why you would have been jealous of seeing me with Lord Holland any more than I would feel jealous to see you with Lucy. It does not signify. Are we not all friends?"

"It may not signify. It may seem entirely unreasonable, but it is what it is. I did not like seeing you with him, and I am not ashamed of admitting it. What I am ashamed of is that my behaviour gave you cause for concern. How can I make amends?"

"It is simple. You must promise never to behave that way again."

"Is that all?"

"Do I have your promise?"

"I shall do my best not to become jealous when I see you with other men. I value your good opinion—more than you know."

"And I yours, although I hardly know why that is the case. Your manner from one moment to the next is so varying as to frustrate me exceedingly. How am I truly to sketch your character when your demeanour fluctuates from warm and amiable to cold and aloof in the blink of an eye?"

"I would by no means suspend any pleasure of yours," he replied. She said no more, and they went down the other dance in silence. They were soon to part when Darcy delayed Elizabeth with an offer to escort her to the beverage table. It was more of a demand than a request, and when Elizabeth glanced around to determine what might have prompted him to do as he did, she espied Miss Bingley hurrying their way. For a moment, Elizabeth was tempted to leave him to Caroline's devices, but she decided nothing he had done warranted such a fate.

After handing her a glass of punch, Mr. Darcy persuaded Elizabeth to accompany him to the balcony. Once outside, Elizabeth breathed in deeply. The balmy air, the muted sounds of the orchestra, and the clouds dancing across the bright full moon conspired to make it the perfect night. Elizabeth was happy to spend time with Mr. Darcy. She felt a certain calm when in his presence, despite her firm resolution at the start of the evening not to be upset should the haughty and aloof Mr. Darcy from the earliest days of her acquaintance be the one who made an appearance at the ball that evening. *This* Mr. Darcy was very agreeable even if he was silent. She felt as though she were the only woman in the room when the two of them danced, for his eyes were only for her.

His wonderfully brilliant eyes.

Elizabeth turned away and fought mightily to keep from smiling in recollection of Betsy's pronouncement that if one were not careful, one might easily drown in Mr. Darcy's eyes.

She was inclined to agree, and it was for that reason that she always found herself tempted to look deeply into his alluring eyes whenever she was afforded a chance.

Everything about this beautiful man tempted her, which explained her even being alone with him at that moment. However, if she were to remain with him, then some conversation needed to be had.

"I find that private balls are much pleasanter than public ones," said Elizabeth.

"I agree."

"Lady Clarissa seems very much in her element. I should imagine she welcomes any opportunity to entertain guests here at Avondale."

"Holland has always said the same of his mother."

"She is so fortunate as to have a house full of guests here at Bosley during a time when one would expect so many to be in London, what with this being the start of the Season."

Darcy said nothing. He turned away and leaned over the balustrade.

"Are you planning to set off for London soon, Mr. Darcy?"

"No." Assuming a more welcoming posture, he motioned for Elizabeth to stand closer to him. "At least, I do not intend to unless I am given a reason."

"Ah, and what reason would compel you to change your plans?"

"Are *you* planning to spend the Season in Town?"

She shrugged. "I am not. I suspect Lady Vanessa does not like Town even though she has not said as much, which suits me just fine. I am perfectly content to remain here in Bosley."

A hint of a smile played across his face, and Elizabeth concluded that he was pleased by her disclosure. "I suppose matters of business keep you here in Bosley, sir. What else might tempt you to forego the chance to partake in the Season?"

"I have several reasons for remaining here—some of them relating to breeding and training and some of them being of a more personal nature."

"Pray you were not vexed that Lord Holland showed me the thoroughbreds you have stabled here at Avondale. Could that have been the reason for your unenthusiastic response the last time I saw you?"

"I confess that I would have liked to have been the one to introduce you to some of my most prized possessions, but as I said, I was jealous of your being with Holland. For one, I was caught completely by surprise. But more important, I did not like seeing you with him."

Her stomach fluttered. How could she not have been flattered that such a man would be bothered enough by the thought of her being with another that he would confess it out loud? "Well then, I should hate to think of you truly suffering on my account, sir, for what bites at one's equanimity more than jealousy? We must endeavour to see that you never feel that way again."

"Are you laughing at me, Miss Bennet?"

"Are you not to be teased, Mr. Darcy?"

"I find it hard to forgive the follies of others when exercised at my expense."

"What a shame, for I dearly love to laugh."

"Well, if that is indeed the case, I will have to allow for exceptions—keeping in mind your good intention."

"Indeed, I would never intentionally cause you any discomfort. You are in no danger from me."

"On the contrary, Miss Bennet. I find I am in grave danger as regards you. However, you will hear no complaints from me."

By now he was standing directly before her—towering over her and peering into her eyes. His avowal, coupled with the soul-searing look on his face, threw Elizabeth's emotions into a frenzy. Elizabeth's heartbeat fluttered. He moistened his lips, encouraging her to do the same. Her heart beat violently against her chest, and her entire body tingled with expectation. *Oh, what a night for a first kiss ever.* He leaned closer—closed his eyes and move closer still, arousing every fibre in her being.

This could be the start of something—something. Reason trumped desire, and Elizabeth eased away.

She turned her head to look away and took a sip of her punch. "I suppose you and I should find our way to the ball-room, sir. Our absence will be duly noted. How will I explain what kept me to my aunt and other inquiring minds?"

Surrendering the battle against his overwhelming need to touch her, Darcy swept a loosened curl behind her ear. "You might say you were availing yourself of the opportunity to sketch my character."

Darcy reached for Elizabeth's hand and bestowed a moist kiss on her palm. "Come, let us return to the ballroom and enjoy another set before supper."

"Two sets, Mr. Darcy! What will people think?"

"Let others think what they will. I am of a mind to sketch *your* character as well, and I am finding that I need more time— the rest of the evening, in fact. I should also hope to spend tomorrow and the day after that in said endeavour. My curiosity, when it comes to you, is insatiable."

Less than a week later, Lady Clarissa once again entertained a house full of dinner guests. To her way of thinking, what was the purpose of such abundance if she could not share it with the people who meant most to her? Very often that meant all the best families in Bosley. After dinner, when everyone was gathered in the grand parlour enjoying one of Lady Clarissa's exhibitions on the pianoforte, Lord Holland saw Miss Bingley standing alone in a corner. By the dour look on her face, she was not happy. He could easily guess what the cause of her distress was. He had yet to notice his friend paying any attention to the young woman during her stay at Avondale. As she was his guest, albeit his uninvited guest, he felt obliged to spend a bit of time with her, especially as her acquaintances were few. He crossed the room with deliberate strides and bowed slightly before her.

"Miss Bingley, how are you this evening?"

"I get along very well, my lord." She plastered a smile on her face. "May I take this time to thank you once again for your kind hospitality towards my brother, Charles, and me?"

"It is my pleasure, madam."

Caroline leaned in conspiratorially. "So, what do you think of our Miss Eliza Bennet, Lord Holland?"

"Miss Bennet is lovely. She is a refreshing change."

"She is different. I will give you that."

"Be careful, Miss Bingley. Your voice rings with disapproval."

"You mistake me, my lord. I simply detect in her none of the evidence of good breeding and taste that renders her suitable for *our* society. She is impertinent in a manner that is hardly attractive, and she has an unrefined air that evidences her lack of accomplishment."

Caroline huffed. "For my own part," she said, "I must confess that I see nothing of beauty in her. Her face is too thin, her complexion has no brilliancy, and her features are not at all handsome. Her nose wants character; there is nothing marked in its lines. Her teeth are tolerable, but not out of the common way. As for her eyes, I can perceive nothing extraordinary in them. They have a sharp, shrewish look, which I do not like at all."

Lord Holland's threshold for tolerating his friend Bingley's sister had always been low, and it was falling even lower by the second. Surely she did not consider such an unflattering comportment to be sufficient means of recommending herself amongst strangers, which is exactly what she was to most of the people assembled at his home that evening. His nettled silence only encouraged her.

"The fact is that she has little to recommend herself except being an excellent walker. What sort of accomplishment is that for a proper young woman?"

Lord Holland directed his gaze to Elizabeth and Darcy standing across the room engaged in what looked like an intimate discourse. Caroline's eyes followed that same path.

"It appears as though not everyone shares your unflattering opinion of the young lady," said his lordship.

"If you are speaking of Mr. Darcy, I must say, I do not know what has gotten into him. He seems captivated by what he described to me as her *fine eyes*."

Lord Holland silently reflected on how much he would love to switch places with Darcy at the moment. "Well, as I said, Miss Bennet is quite lovely. She is, in fact, one of the loveliest women of my acquaintance."

His avowal immediately met with Caroline's displeasure, judging by the look she bestowed. "Oh, please, my lord. Do not tell me that you, too, are taken in by her low, country arts and allurements." She threw a disgusted glance at Elizabeth. "I wager neither you nor Mr. Darcy would be half so impressed if you really knew what she is about."

"What have you to accuse Miss Bennet of, Miss Bingley?"

"There are many things about the woman that are in stark contrast to the facade afforded by her presence in Bosley, but as I am not one to gossip, you shall not hear any of that from me." Caroline curtsied, signalling her intention to say no more on the subject at that time. "Pardon me, my lord." With that, she went away.

Caroline did not get very far. Lady Vanessa, who had been standing close enough to hear the last of Caroline's words to Lord Holland, beckoned the young lady's attention. She approached Caroline. "Miss Bingley, shall we take a turn about the room?"

Caroline readily acquiesced, and Lady Vanessa and she began walking arm in arm. "How are you enjoying your stay in Bosley?"

"I find the society to be quite lovely, your ladyship."

"Excellent. I am sure you have observed by now that we are a very close-knit society. In fact, Lady Clarissa and I are family. What is more, she is my dearest friend."

"Lady Clarissa is someone whom I have come to appreciate as well."

"I should warn you that Lady Clarissa is not one to tolerate dissension, nor does she countenance the idea of anyone disparaging her family. I could not help but hear your uncharitable remarks about my niece, whom her ladyship also regards as family. Whatever it is that you consider as sufficient motive to demean my niece, I suggest you take a good look in the mirror. You might reflect upon your own family legacy."

Lady Vanessa cast a disheartened glance towards the part of the room where Darcy and Elizabeth sat. "No doubt your distaste is fuelled by your displeasure in seeing the object of your desire bestowing his attentions towards my niece, but that is hardly any of my concern. I only care about my niece's felicity, hence the purpose of this little tête-à-tête. Unless you desire an abrupt end to your acceptance amongst our society, I advise you to mind your tongue."

Chapter 7

May Take Liberties

Darcy approached Lord Holland and Elizabeth, threw the former a cursory glance and bowed slightly towards the latter. "I shall wait for you by my curricle, Miss Bennet."

When Darcy walked away, Elizabeth looked at the viscount apologetically. "That is what I was about to tell you. I have already accepted Mr. Darcy's invitation to ride in his carriage. Please understand."

The idea and the planning of a country outing had been his lordship's doing. He and his mother had invited many of the neighbours to accompany them: the Davidsons, the Lancasters, and of course Lady Vanessa and Elizabeth, and finally Charles and Caroline Bingley as they were still his guests, and they were not showing any indication of taking their leave.

He held up his hand, his countenance speaking to his disappointment. "You owe me no explanation. I only hope you know what you are about."

"Pray, what does that mean?"

Lord Holland narrowed his eyes and punctured his voice with ire. "Do you suppose for one instant that he will fall in love with you, Miss Bennet?"

Elizabeth liked Lord Holland very much, but this was a side of him that met with her displeasure. Unable to fashion a response that would satisfy either of them, Elizabeth remained silent.

He crossed his arms. "I have known Darcy his entire adult life. He will not forget what is expected of him and fall in love with you. It is not in his nature."

Elizabeth had heard enough. She dipped a quick curtsy. "Pardon me, my lord." She then promptly escaped his company.

Darcy was speaking with his friend Charles Bingley when Elizabeth arrived and took her place by his side.

Bingley greeted her with a smile. "Miss Bennet, it is a pleasure to see you this morning."

"I thank you, sir. I am very happy to see you as well."

The charming Mr. Bingley glanced about and took in all there was to see before returning his attention to Elizabeth. "Indeed, the sun is beaming warmly upon us, the birds are singing, the flowers are awash in colours, and the weather is pleasant and inviting. What a perfect day this is for a country outing."

By the looks of Mr. Darcy's sudden change in countenance, Elizabeth supposed he disagreed. He looked as though he were standing in the middle of a road with a team of wild stallions closing in on him. Elizabeth did not even have to turn around to discern the cause, for a piercing voice rang out from across the yard. She did look, and she saw Caroline Bingley headed their way with her hand atop her garish feathery bonnet to keep it from falling to the ground amidst her haste.

Darcy claimed Elizabeth's hand. "Come, Miss Bennet. Your chariot waits." Before she knew what she was about, he had ushered her away with nary a word of pardon to Mr. Bingley.

Darcy handed Elizabeth into his curricle, and he quickly strode to the other side and boarded the vehicle as well. Once he made certain Elizabeth was seated comfortably, Darcy raced ahead of the others and chose an alternate path than had been agreed upon, thus arriving at the destination well in advance of the rest of the party.

Darcy handed her down from the curricle, and Elizabeth looked about, full of wonder and excitement over all she saw. The whole country about them abounded in beautiful walks, and Elizabeth's eagerness to set out and explore them could scarcely be contained despite Darcy's half-hearted attempt to do just that. Once he had seen to the security of his curricle and his horses, he and Elizabeth set off together.

Not long after everyone had established themselves under the outdoor tents that had been arranged for their dining comfort, Lady Vanessa approached Lord Holland, who was standing away from the gathering. "Where is my niece? Pray tell me again how is it that she came to ride in Mr. Darcy's curricle?" Her ladyship shielded her eyes from the glaring sun as she surveyed the surroundings. "She said nothing to me about riding with Mr. Darcy—with no chaperone. I thought she was to ride with you."

His lordship shrugged. "It seems he asked her first. As you must have surmised, his choice of conveyance lent itself to only two occupants."

"That is no excuse. I wish Elizabeth had ridden in the carriage with you as we had planned. Obstinate, headstrong girl! Oh, where do you suppose she is?"

"You need not worry, Lady Vanessa. You know your niece. She likely took one look at the magnificent grounds and set off to explore. My friend Darcy will see that she comes to no harm."

"I know you believe your friend is very responsible, and I know he comes from a decent family, but what do we really know about him? Even you will admit he has gone out of his way to keep himself to himself. During those times he has called on us at Barrington, he has been quiet and taciturn. I hardly know what to make of him."

"That is his way. I know him well enough not to be concerned; however, if it will help to ease your mind, I will seek out the two of them and escort them back to the party."

"Would you, my dear? It would mean the world to me." Lord Holland was gone directly—his mind consumed with what he might do if all of his reassurances to Lady Vanessa proved false.

If only Miss Bennet knew how much I care for her, then would she bestow her smiles as liberally upon me as she does towards Darcy? I would give anything to have her look at me the way she looks at him. She cannot possibly know what is in store for her if she supposes Darcy's interest in her is more than fleeting—a mere diversion.

Lord Holland recalled the wrath that always commandeered Miss Bingley's composure whenever she saw Darcy and Elizabeth together. *While it is true that I have never seen him as attentive to any woman as he is to Miss Bennet, I have to suppose it is merely a means to frustrate Miss Bingley. Darcy's family fully expects him to marry his cousin—everyone who knows anything at all about the proud Fitzwilliams knows that.*

Exhilarated by the fresh, open air, Elizabeth's hurried steps by far outpaced Mr. Darcy's. She turned back to her companion, who was intent upon a leisurely stroll. She was tempted to walk back to him, take him by the arm, and pull him along. "Mr. Darcy, if you do not walk faster, then we shall never take in all there is to see before it is time to join the others."

He maintained his slow, steady pace, thus obliging Elizabeth to do the same. "I do not recall you ever being this enthusiastic about a walk, Miss Bennet."

"When I am at home in Hertfordshire, I enjoy nothing better than a long, solitary ramble about the countryside. It is but one of the things I miss most about being away from home. My favourite escape is Oakham Mount. I walked there whenever I could."

"I hope you will take me there one day."

"Oh, but surely you miss Derbyshire as well, Mr. Darcy."

"I do."

"I have heard it said that Derbyshire boasts some of the most magnificent vistas in the country."

"It is quite splendid: breath-taking mountains, majestic lakes, and flowing rivers. Pemberley, my home, is especially beautiful at this time of year. There are secluded paths along winding streams that go on for miles. I can hardly wait for you to see it. You will be delighted."

Indeed, she could half imagine the splendours he foretold. *But what can he mean in suggesting I might one day behold it with delight?* "You envision me one day visiting your home in Derbyshire, Mr. Darcy?"

He ceased walking and encouraged her to stand still. "I do." Darcy lifted Elizabeth's hand, slowly slipped off her glove, and placed a moist kiss on her palm. Their eyes met and held fast in each other's until Elizabeth felt a titillating heat spread throughout her body, and she looked away. Darcy said, "Although, I fear once you see the lanes about the park, I may not see you half as much as I would wish."

Recollection of being this close to him the night of the Avondale ball took hold of Elizabeth, and she suffered a frisson of nervous anticipation. Reclaiming her glove, she stepped away. "Do you often entertain guests at Pemberley, sir? I mean to say when you are there."

"Yes, when I return to Pemberley, I very often arrive with a large party. In fact, Charles Bingley and his relations are frequent guests."

"I no longer have cause to wonder—" Not wishing to speak out of turn, Elizabeth halted her speech.

"Wonder what, Miss Bennet?"

"You might consider me a bit presumptuous when you hear what I have to say."

"You are free to say whatever you wish to me, Miss Bennet.

You will find that I am not easily offended."

This, she considered sufficient encouragement to speak at liberty. "I now understand Miss Bingley's fondness for you. Perhaps the lady harbours hopes of being something other than a frequent guest."

Darcy said nothing. His puzzled expression encouraged her to continue. "Surely you are aware of her feelings for you. One would have to be daft not to."

"When you couch your opinion in those terms, I am obliged to answer you in the affirmative."

"You mean to say you *are* aware of the lady's feelings?"

"I am; however, she tries too hard, and trying too hard to capture my attention, or any man's notice for that matter, is the surest way to discourage it. Besides, even a shy Miss Bingley would fail to garner my heart."

"So, Mr. Darcy, you have given your heart to another?"

"I want to." He took her hand again, led her to a grassy knoll, and encouraged her to sit with him. He traced his fingers along her chin. "Do you know how amazing you are? I believe you are a goddess sent from the heavens to rob me of my composure and render me incapable of thinking a single thought that does not centre on you.

"Being with you like this seems right as if it is what I was meant to be doing. You must feel it as well." His deep voice struck all the right cords, rendering Elizabeth speechless amidst the rush of heat flooding her entire being.

"You need not to say a word, for I already know the answer." Darcy took out his pocket knife. He threaded a lock of Elizabeth's hair around his finger.

"Mr. Darcy?"

How he wanted to lean in and bestow a tender kiss upon her lips. Instead, he leaned down and spoke softly in her ear. "The evening of the ball, I spoke of being in grave danger as regards you, but I did not complete the sentiment. What I should have said is I am in grave danger of surrendering my heart to you. You are more important to me than you know." He breathed in the fresh scent of her hair—pleasingly awash in lavender. "May I?"

The warm, sweet caress of his breath against her skin robbed her of her composure. *What could be his meaning?* He took her silence as acquiescence. His ardent purpose completed, he folded his precious treasure up in his crisp white handkerchief, kissed it, and placed it in his breast pocket.

"Now that you have a lock of my hair, what do you intend to do with it, sir?"

"What else but carry it with me—here," he rested his hand over his chest, "close to my heart as a means of having you with me everywhere I go?"

What they had done had exceeded the bounds of decorum. What a scandal it would have been were they discovered. The taking of one's hair was as good as a commitment, yet no true declaration of intention had been made. Elizabeth endeavoured mightily to silence the cautioning whispers that admonished her for allowing Mr. Darcy such liberties. Even now, she wanted to kick herself for shying away from what would have been her first kiss that night on the balcony during the Holland ball. *What is the harm, especially as there is no one other than the two of us to bear witness to what took place?*

Chapter 8

Reason to Fear

D arcy and his groom were embroiled in deep discussion in
the stable, when out of nowhere, Lord Holland stormed up
to them. His jaws twitching, he directed a menacing glower at
the groom. "Leave us!"

The groom, rather wishing to take his orders from his master, walked away after Darcy ceded permission. Darcy could
never recall seeing his lordship short-tempered and dismissive.

His posture threatening, Lord Holland soon answered the
unasked question of what had brought about his raging attitude. "Your unguarded behaviour towards Miss Bennet is
inexcusable."

Darcy squarely met Lord Holland's gaze. "I beg your pardon?"

"I saw the two of you together earlier today."

"Then perhaps you should have made your presence

known."

"Had I done so, I would have embarrassed the young woman. She does not deserve to be humiliated, nor does she deserve to be hurt."

"I would never hurt her."

"You say that now, but there will come a time when you will, and you know of what I speak. I only pray the damage is not severe."

"My relationship with Miss Bennet does not concern you. That being said, she understands my intentions."

"Then you have asked her to accept your hand?" Lord Holland did not wait for an answer. He knew his friend very well. "Of course you have not, and you never will."

"When have you ever known me to trifle with a young woman's affections?"

"I know you have left many women heartbroken in your wake."

"None of it my own doing—I shall not assume responsibility for every young woman whose path has crossed with my own and who found herself wishing to be the next mistress of Pemberley. What Elizabeth and I share is different, and you had better respect that. I am no fool to the way you look at her."

Refusing to back down, Lord Holland squared his shoulders and curled his hands into fists. "Perhaps you truly believe your intentions towards the young lady are honourable. You have delayed your departure by more than a few weeks and on more than one occasion, ostensibly to oversee your financial interests, when you and I know the true reason. However, we also know it is solely a matter of time before you do take your leave—rendering the young woman broken-hearted. When you do, I promise I will be here to pick up the pieces and help mend it back together."

Just under a week had passed, and once again the Barrington Hall party were dinner guests at Avondale. This vexed Caroline exceedingly, but as she was a guest herself, she dared not complain. How delighted Caroline was that Eliza Bennet was not in the drawing room when Darcy made his way there with the rest of the gentlemen to join the ladies after dinner port. Seizing the opportunity, Caroline saddled up beside him and persuaded him to come and sit beside her in the farthest corner of the room. They had spent little time together as had always been their wont whenever at Pemberley and in London, and she meant to rectify that injustice that evening, her last evening at Avondale before she and her brother took their leave of Bosley.

Caroline still smarted over an earlier remark Darcy had made about his mind being agreeably engaged in meditating on the immense pleasure that a pair of fine eyes in the face of a pretty woman could bestow, when all Caroline meant to do was tempt him to sing her own praises.

Caroline was tired of Darcy being in the dark about the Bennets of Hertfordshire. If she did nothing else, she meant to enlighten him, even at the risk of raising his ire. Then again it would never come to that, for surely he would thank her once he had time to consider the service she had rendered on his behalf.

"It is such a pleasure to be once again amongst society after so long a spell in the country amidst the savages. Has Charles spoken to you of any of the people in Hertfordshire? While they will boast of their varied society, I found little to be pleased with and very little of good taste and decorum with which to please myself."

Darcy shifted restlessly, but he said nothing. He accepted a glass of champagne from a passing footman.

"There was one family in particular whose lowly manners I found especially disagreeable. Had you accepted Charles's invitation and joined us during last Michaelmas, I am certain you would have agreed. The mother and the two youngest daughters were ridiculous, vulgar, and crude, and their fashion sense was that of barbarians."

"Surely you did not expect to find your neighbours donned in the latest London fashions."

"I most certainly did. Their only hope in life is to make favourable connections. What hope does one have if one fails to present oneself well? Not that it would signify in their cases. The family has no outward appearance of wealth or connections, and prepare yourself; although the father, who is at times as crass as the mother, fancies himself a gentleman, he went and married a woman whose family is in trade—merchants and country lawyers and the like.

"One would wish with all one's heart that the poor creatures were well settled. But with such a father and mother and with such low connections, I am afraid there is no chance of it. What say you, Mr. Darcy? Without knowing all the particulars, tell me what do you suppose are the daughters' chances of securing favourable matches in such circumstances?"

"I suppose it must very materially lessen their chance of marrying men of any consideration in the world," said Darcy, "that is, if what you say is true."

"Why, Mr. Darcy, when have you known me to utter untruths?"

Bingley joined them. "I do not ever recall you commanding Darcy's attention for so long a time, Caroline. What are the two of you discussing?"

"Your sister was just telling me about the dire circumstances of one of your Hertfordshire neighbours, and the unlikely prospect of them securing favourable alliances as a result."

Bingley wrung his hands. "The family Caroline speaks of is the Bennets of Longbourn. You have met Miss Bennet. I am sure you have discerned that my sister exaggerates."

Having just taken a sip of his drink, Darcy nearly coughed it up. "The Bennets?"

"Yes, and as I have told both my sisters, if the Bennet daughters had uncles enough to fill all of Cheapside, it would not make them one jot less agreeable." He raked his fingers through his hair and released a heavy sigh. "Really, Caroline, must you continue to disparage the Bennets? Why must you go on and on? What can any of that have to do with you?"

To this speech, she made no answer. Satisfied she had persuaded Darcy to give voice to the very objection he would have once he knew Eliza Bennet's true circumstances, Caroline did not see the need to say more. Even a connection with Lady Vanessa would not be enough to remove the stench of such horrible relations as were afforded by Eliza Bennet's mother's side of the family. Darcy, Bingley, and Caroline were embroiled in uncomfortable silence when Elizabeth entered the room.

Caroline nodded. "There is Miss Eliza Bennet now." Darcy turned in the direction Caroline had indicated. She lowered her voice to a half whisper. "I am afraid, Mr. Darcy, that this information has rather affected your admiration of her fine eyes."

Darcy had heard enough of Miss Bingley's venomous words. "Pardon me, Bingley, Miss Bingley." With a curt bow he walked away, but rather than join Elizabeth, he quit the room.

Outside alone on the balcony, his mind was a tumultuous mixture of ire and confusion. How on earth was it possible that the family Miss Bingley described was the family of the woman who now owned his heart? *Low connections, low morals—how is this to be endured?* He and Elizabeth had spoken at length about her eldest sister, but rarely did she even mention the younger ones. As for her connections, with Lady Vanessa being her aunt—her father's sister—Darcy never considered not all her relatives were equally as lofty.

Elizabeth found Darcy looking grave and concerned. "Sir, I must apologise; my aunt is feeling quite indisposed. She has indicated her desire to return home, and she asks that I join her."

"Of course."

She folded her arms under her breast and regarded him pointedly, yet her playful manner would not be repressed. "I expected you to show more concern than this; after all, who shall protect you from the likes of Miss Bingley when I am gone?"

"You must forgive me. I have recently received rather disturbing news. I am merely distracted. Of course, I am disappointed not to spend as much time in your company as I had hoped this evening. You cannot imagine how disappointed I am."

"Then shall I expect to see you tomorrow?"

"Yes, yes, of course. I will call on you."

Puzzled, Elizabeth walked away. No touch of his hand, no brush of his lips across her knuckles, nothing—save a distant, unreadable stare. *Will I ever grow accustomed to his changeable moods?*

Elizabeth's intercourse on the balcony with Mr. Darcy left her in a foul mood. Now it was her turn to be silent and grave on the carriage ride home. While the butler, the housekeeper, and Lady Vanessa's maid made a commotion attending to their mistress's comfort, Elizabeth quickly made her way up the stairs to her room.

She drifted over to the window and peered out at the low-hanging moon. After a few minutes, she sighed heavily. There really was only one way for her to sort out the enigma that was Mr. Darcy, and that was to commit her thoughts to paper. *If I am quick about it, I shall be done before Betsy arrives.*

Elizabeth took a seat at her desk, retrieved the key from the safe place she had detected just underneath, unlocked the drawer, and retrieved a fresh piece of paper. Once her pen was mended, she began.

Just as I was beginning to imagine that I knew and understood Mr. Darcy perfectly well, I discovered this evening that I do not know him at all. I surely do not comprehend the gentleman. This evening at Avondale, he was aloof and inattentive—nothing at all like the amiable and caring man he was as recently as this morning during our riding lesson. Such varying behaviour is exceedingly puzzling and more than a little vexing. If I were so inclined, I would have to ask: Is such a man to be trusted with one's heart?

Betsy entered the room while Elizabeth was about to begin her next sentence. She showed a healthy interest in Elizabeth's wont of writing at such an hour, and once again, she offered to deliver the letter downstairs when Elizabeth was done. This time Elizabeth's annoyance with Mr. Darcy manifested itself to her maid's detriment. "Betsy, for the last time, I do not require you to deliver my letter. I am more than capable of handling my own affairs!"

Betsy recoiled. Elizabeth grew contrite. The last thing she meant to do was raise her voice. Betsy was simply doing her job. She looked at herself in the mirror and studied her reflection. *What has come over me?*

"Betsy, pray you will forgive me for my outburst. The truth is the missive that I spend countless hours pouring my heart into is not truly a missive at all, for I never intend to send it to anyone."

"Then would you say it is more of a journal?"

"It might be better described as such. The fact is, I believe I would be lost without it."

When Betsy was gone, Elizabeth reflected on what her writings truly signified. The truth was that as much as she wished to move on from her eldest sister's death, even now she was incapable of saying goodbye. The letters that bore evidence of her deepest held secrets, letters that were never meant to be sent were her means of clinging to her sister. They served as a constant in her life. Now she was at a crossroads. She had never meant to be anything other than friends with Mr. Darcy, thinking as she did that she could never truly give her heart over to anyone. To do so would mean opening herself up to the possibility of suffering the pain akin to that which she felt in losing Jane. And that was something she was simply not ready to do, or was she? Rather than go to bed, Elizabeth picked up the candle from her bedside table, slowly drifted back to her writing desk, settled in her chair, and reached for her pen. *It is going to be a long night.*

As soon as proper decorum allowed the next morning, Darcy called on Elizabeth. Having attended to those pleasantries meant to satisfy her aunt of the notion of his even being there, Darcy invited Elizabeth to walk with him in the garden.

They walked for a time in complete silence while he tried to decide how best to approach the subject that had robbed him of his composure most of the night. At length, he spoke. "You rarely speak of your family. I should like to know more about them."

"Indeed, but surely you will concede that you are equally silent on the matter of your own family, sir?"

"My family's history reads much like an opened book, but I will gladly satisfy any curiosity you may have. Ask me anything?"

"I will confess that Lady Vanessa shared a bit of your family's history with me. I know that your uncle is Lord Edward Fitzwilliam, the Earl of Matlock. She spoke of your late parents as well. I will take this time to say that I am sorry for your loss."

"I lost both of my parents many years ago—my mother when I was young and my father after I became of age. When he died, he designated the care of my younger sister, Georgiana, to me and my older cousin Colonel Richard Fitzwilliam. It is a circumstance that grieved my aunt and uncle as much as my father's passing, for neither of them considered me ready to assume the management of my estate as well as the guardianship of my sister. In fairness to them, I did stumble along the way, but my sister and I have both learned from the experience, and we are well on our way to putting it behind us completely."

"Is your sister out in Society?"

"No—heaven forbid! She has endured so much for someone so young, and I dare say she has got over the most trying age. Still, she is not yet seventeen. She has ample time."

"I am afraid I cannot say the same of my own sisters, for they are all out, even the youngest who is not sixteen. I have always supposed that it would be rather unfair to deny the younger sisters their chance for gaiety merely on the basis of the older sisters not being married."

"Surely everyone's situation is different. My sister's not being out has nothing at all to do with an older sister's not being married, for she has none. No, the reason she is not out has more to do with age and maturity. I believe she will be ready in a couple of years. Until then, she shall continue to benefit from the wisdom of her companion, a Mrs. Annesley, who resides with Georgiana."

"Then I take it she does not live with you at Pemberley."

"No, she often visits—that is, when I am in Derbyshire, but she has her own establishment in Town." Anxious to get to the heart of what was weighing upon him most, Darcy said, "We have spoken enough about my family. Tell me more about yours. What are they like?"

"Well, other than Lady Vanessa who married most advantageously, I can hardly boast of connections as lofty as yours. Truth be told, if you are anything at all like Lady Vanessa, which I pray you are not, then you will be appalled to know that my mother's father was in trade, and my uncles are in trade. One is a Meryton attorney, the other a merchant who lives in Cheapside." She crossed her arms and looked him squarely in his eyes. "Now, hate me if you dare."

Darcy unfolded her arms and took her hand in his. "I could never hate you, and you know that."

After a moment, Elizabeth pulled away her hand. "I also will add that my father's estate is entailed to the male line of his family. I have a ridiculous cousin, Mr. Collins, who pursuant to my father's passing can turn us all out into the hedgerows as soon as he pleases. It is for this reason that my mama is determined that we all should find husbands as soon as can be, and it is a factor in my sisters being out at such early ages.

"That brings me to an account of my sisters. My father proclaims them to be the silliest creatures in all of England. I give you leave to read in his sentiments whatever you will. My sister Mary is an ardent reader and other than practice diligently on the pianoforte, there is nothing she would rather do. My younger sisters Kitty and Lydia are nothing at all like Mary, for they would consider it a pain to open a book and a punishment to go near the pianoforte. Their idea of accomplishment is walking to Meryton in search of the latest news.

"With the militia's being encamped there, they are known to venture into Meryton each day, for they find nothing more pleasing than dashing officers in red coats. They are especially fond of an officer who hails from Derbyshire—a Lieutenant George Wickham." Elizabeth stopped, recollecting that said gentleman had boasted of living at Pemberley. *Why have I not made the connection before?*

"Wickham!" Darcy spat the appellation. "I know him quite well."

"Everyone who has met him thinks he is amiable."

"Mr. Wickham is blessed with such happy manners as may ensure his making friends—whether he may be equally capable of retaining them is less certain."

"Oh, my! You sound as though the gentleman has been so unlucky as to lose your friendship."

"Indeed, he has. My good opinion, once lost, is lost forever." Darcy folded his arms over his chest and looked away. "However, that is a matter I have no wish to discuss."

Elizabeth moved closer and placed her hand on Darcy's arm. "You will forgive me for introducing such a delicate subject. I had no idea of your feelings against the gentleman."

"Of course you did not. How could you have known? As for my forgiving you," he claimed both her hands, "I believe I would forgive you anything."

The couple stared into each other's eyes as if searching for answers of what happens next.

Darcy wanted nothing more than to kiss her. To relish the taste of her lips—sweet, unpractised, just as the first kiss with the woman he loved ought to be. A kiss meant to do more than sate his increasing desire for her; it meant to serve as an avowal of his commitment to her—an unspoken promise.

He placed his hands about her neck, gently massaged her under her chin as he lifted her head, and leaned in.

Wanting more than anything to know what it was like to be kissed by him, desperately wanting to surrender to her body's demands to be near him, and wanting nothing to take away from the magic of the moment, she moistened her lips and closed her eyes. And in an instant, she knew what it was like to be swept off her feet, intoxicated with bliss.

The gentle touch of his lips upon hers was tender; it was undemanding, and it was perfect.

Chapter 9

A Lively Mind

A week had passed, during which Darcy had spent far less time with Elizabeth than he would have wished. It could not be helped. Matters of business had demanded his attention most of his days, and the few nights they were in company, it seemed Lady Vanessa had been intent upon taking up the role as chaperone for her niece. The one consolation he had was that he had managed to secure a few moments alone with Elizabeth the prior evening, and he had promised her a riding lesson in two days, as soon as his business with the head groomsman at Avondale and his solicitor from London was settled.

Little did he suspect that his plans were about to change. Darcy had just returned from the stable and was preparing to order a hot, steaming bath when his cousin Colonel Richard Fitzwilliam, who had arrived at Avondale without notice, and as best Darcy could tell, without a proper invitation from the

Hollands, walked into his room. The gentlemen shook hands. "Richard, my friend, I did not expect to see you here. What brings you to Bosley?"

"The better question is what are you doing here? I thought your purpose in coming here was to acquire a couple of thoroughbreds, not establish a second home."

"My standards are exacting when it comes to the proper care of my thoroughbreds. It does take time to assure that my interests are protected."

Richard's countenance clouded. "Is there a problem with the quality of Avondale's stables?"

"No, all is well in that regard."

"Then what is it? I was forced to endure our dear aunt Lady Catherine's company and her ceaseless complaints over your inattention for nearly a week before I simply decided that enough was enough."

"My reasons for foregoing the trip to Rosings are of a personal nature. Besides, with the upcoming race in Richland, I thought I would call on her ladyship and Cousin Anne when I arrived in Kent."

"Oh, then you do intend to attend the race?"

"Of course, I mean to attend the race. Why would I not? I have attended every year since I was of age, even before I became a member of the Jockey's Club and owner of a stable of prize-winning thoroughbreds."

Richard arched his brow. "Our aunt argues that you have never missed your annual visit to Rosings Park."

"Those are entirely different matters, and you know it."

"Pray enlighten me, if you will. Familial obligation has always ranked as high on your list of priorities as horse racing, yet you seemed to have allowed the former to fall by the wayside while you languish about in Bosley."

"For heaven's sake, Richard, if I did not know better, I would think Lady Catherine sent you here to do her bidding in the never-ending campaign to make me feel guilty."

"Truth be told, I am here on her ladyship's behalf. She assigned me with the task of coming to Bosley and lulling you away from whatever it is that keeps you here so that you might spend time at Rosings both before and after the race."

Darcy covered his face with both hands and massaged his forehead. "What is the urgency?"

"Lady Catherine fully expects that if you wait until after the Richland race to call on her, it will amount to no more than a cursory visit. She knows the Waltham Mile is soon thereafter." Richard reached into his pocket, retrieved a letter, and handed it to Darcy.

"What is this?"

"Lady Catherine asked me to give you this."

"Have you any idea what it entails?"

"She said I was to place it in your hands."

Darcy tore open the missive. His temper flared with each second he read it. He folded it when he was done.

"Do not keep me in suspense."

Darcy handed the letter back to his cousin so he might read everything her ladyship had to say for himself. Impatient to discuss the matter, he did not wait for Richard to finish. "It seems our aunt is considering selling Hercules."

"Is that not Grandfather's prize-winning bay? I know he is retired from racing, but I always supposed he would remain in the Fitzwilliam family."

"Exactly; she knows I would never countenance his being sold. She says she will offer me first right of refusal, with one stipulation: I must come to Kent and negotiate face to face."

"Our aunt drives a hard bargain. You must know she intends that you should attend your *would-be* betrothed in a manner befitting a rich young heiress while you are there."

"Richard, you know I never promised our family that I would honour their wishes that I should marry Anne."

"I do not know that I do. Surely you have never said as much to her ladyship."

"Well, the time has come for me to do just that."

"Why now, after you have suffered all these years of essentially ignoring the matter?" Sudden realisation graced his countenance. Richard gaped. "Could this be the reason for your protracted stay in Bosley? Has some young filly finally captured the heart of the elusive Mr. Darcy of Pemberley and Derbyshire?"

"I am quite certain I would never describe the young woman in those terms and neither should you." Just thinking of the set-down his cousin would receive if Elizabeth knew he had described her in such terms brought a smile to Darcy's face. "Richard, I am eager for you to meet her. She is charming, witty, and I would add one of the handsomest women of my acquaintance."

"Does this paragon of virtue have a name?"

"She is Miss Elizabeth Bennet of Longbourn in Hertfordshire."

"Longbourn," Richard paused. "Hertfordshire ... I seem to recall our aunt's parson speaking at length about said estate. His name is William Collins. I gather he is the heir apparent. His bride also hails from Hertfordshire. Do you suppose there is a connection?"

"No doubt there is a connection. Miss Bennet has told me that her father's estate is entailed."

"Well what do you know! This young lady is related to our aunt's parson. Imagine how Lady Catherine will carry on once she learns that bit of information."

"All of Miss Bennet's connections are not as low as that, I assure you. She now resides here in Bosley with her aunt Lady Vanessa Barrett."

"What are her other relations? What do you know about her father, her mother, and her siblings?"

"I confess not to have met any of them." *Judging by Caroline Bingley's unflattering opinion, I am not certain I truly wish to.* The mere memory of her was sufficient to make him cringe. "However, Miss Bennet has told me about them, just as I have discussed all of you with her." Darcy recounted parts of Elizabeth's account of her family to Richard: the tragic loss of her most beloved older sister, the absurdities of the younger sisters, the nervousness of the mother, and the proclivities of the father to laugh at them all in their turn while shielding himself from the ridiculousness of it all in the quiet sanctuary of his library.

"What of her father's fortune? If his estate is entailed, how does that bode for his wife and daughters?"

"I confess to being surprised by your callous attitude, Richard, what with your being a second son."

"Ah, yes, a second son indeed, but being the second son of an earl surely must have its advantages what with my being only a heartbeat away from the right of ascension."

"I would hope Lord Robert is unaware of your philosophy."

"Trust me, he knows my sentiments. Even as a mere second son, our family's expectations as regards my alliance are high. I am expected to marry a woman with her own fortune. Let us say that Anne was not the family's choice for you, surely your own choice of a bride can be no less, even if you *are* so very rich."

"I am my own master. At the end of the day, it matters not to me what our family expects. I will choose my own bride. As for their expectations of an alliance with Anne, I will travel to Kent ahead of the race. I will settle this matter once and for all. Then I shall have no impediments whatsoever to keep me from properly declaring my intentions to Miss Bennet."

"My God, man, what are you saying?"

"I care deeply for her. She shall be the next mistress of Pemberley—if she will have me."

"I am sure this news will come as a surprise to our family, most particularly Lady Catherine and possibly Anne as well."

"Hence the twofold purpose in my travelling to Kent. I shall clarify matters with Lady Catherine once and for all."

"Then you surely intend to marry this Miss Bennet?"

"Certainly, but even if that were not the case, telling our aunt that I have no intention of ever marrying Anne is the thing to do. I should have put a stop to that foolishness years ago."

The following morning, Mr. Darcy brought Colonel Fitzwilliam with him when he called at Barrington Hall. The colonel was about thirty. He was not handsome, but in person and address, he was most truly the gentleman. When the introductions were made, Colonel Fitzwilliam directly entered into conversation with the readiness and ease of a well-bred man and talked very pleasantly.

Having greeted everyone with his usual reserve, Darcy seemed contented to have his cousin carry on the bulk of the conversation. The gentleman did so with alacrity.

"Colonel Fitzwilliam, I pray you will enjoy our rather limited society, what with so many of our friends having sojourned to London for the Season," said Elizabeth after a lull in the conversation.

"As pleasing a prospect as that would be, I am unable to offer you assurances. We leave tomorrow."

"*We*, sir? I was not aware you had travelling companions. I should have loved to make their acquaintance."

"I speak of Darcy and me." The colonel's pronouncement unsettled Darcy's calm demeanour, but he said nothing.

Both ladies' voices rang out in startled unison. "So soon?"

A quiet disturbance settled upon the room. Richard stood to take his leave and said his goodbyes and was gone directly.

The quietness in the room subsequent to Richard's hasty departure was nothing in comparison to the silence that accompanied Darcy and Elizabeth on their walk to the garden. The farther they walked, the more she considered the odd confluence of events of late. She had sensed him pulling away gradually, and now he was leaving. Elizabeth thought back to the self-satisfied look upon Caroline Bingley's face her last night at Avondale when she informed Elizabeth that she would find Mr. Darcy on the balcony. *No doubt she was the one who poisoned his thoughts against me. That was over a week ago, and he has been behaving aloof and taciturn ever since. His cousin's coming here affords him a most convenient excuse to do that which he has been planning all along.*

As they had been walking for a time and he had yet to offer an explanation for the sudden turn of events, Elizabeth put forth her own. "It has occurred to me that your regard for me has lessened appreciably since you learned about my family." She raised her head in defiance. "You would never admit it, but I cannot help thinking it is true. Now your own relation has arrived in Bosley, and you are prepared to take your leave the very next day."

He bestowed a look of utter astonishment. "I shall not ascribe to the sentiments you describe as being my own, and I certainly shall not account for them as though they were." Darcy felt his patience waning. He had expected her to be disappointed, but certainly had not expected to defend his decision to leave. When did he ever have to justify any of his actions to anyone? Frustration crept into his speech. "You talk as if I wish to be parted from you when it is simply not true. This is how it is, Elizabeth. My plans were fixed long before we met. You cannot imagine how many times I have delayed my departure already so I might continue to see you each day. As soon as my business is done, I shall return to Bosley—to you."

"To me, Mr. Darcy?" Elizabeth huffed. "Do you suppose I am one of your possessions?"

"I never said you were. Why would you even suggest such a thing?"

"Then why treat me as such ... as if I were a possession that you might place on a shelf while you attend to other diversions with the expectation that you will find said prize just where you left it when it suits you."

"Those are your sentiments, not mine. You reside here in Bosley. Is it unreasonable for me to assume that you will be here when I return?"

"You talk as if you plan to have me sit idly by the window and patiently await your return."

"No—not idly; I suppose you might do any number of things: read, walk, paint screens ... whatever accomplished young women do."

Wanting to erase the pain of disappointment from her eyes, Darcy reached out for her, but she jerked away. "Do not touch me!"

"Elizabeth, you are not being fair." He raked his fingers through his hair and breathed a beleaguered sigh. His voice was heavy with emotion. "Am I to disregard all my prior commitments? I have obligations that demand that I leave."

"Of course, you must do what you must to satisfy your obligations and prior commitments, sir, but why did you make no mention of either of these things before? When you spoke of foregoing the London Season, you led me to believe you were to remain here in Bosley."

"I can see there is no reasoning with you on this matter. The fact is I have changed my plans."

Elizabeth sucked in several deep breaths in an attempt to reclaim her equanimity. Feelings akin to those she suffered when she lost her beloved sister Jane began to encroach upon her. For a while, Mr. Darcy had made her forget what it was like to suffer such heartache. She was beginning to cast off the cloak she had woven in order that she might endure the pain of losing her sister. With him, she had been willing to open her heart—to trust.

For months after losing her dear sister, she had promised she would never suffer a similar pain again. *What better way to protect oneself against the pain of heartbreak than never to expose one's heart at all?* Recognising that she had been on the verge of surrendering her heart to Mr. Darcy, Elizabeth was relieved it had not got that far. She desperately wanted to believe that it was better that she had insisted upon protecting her heart even though her heart was whispering a different refrain.

I will not debate this matter with him. I do not need this. Mr. Darcy made me no promises. If I trusted him, it is merely a sign of my weakness and lack of steadfastness to my own resolve. Her disappointment was evident, and she was angry with herself because of it.

She started feeling constricted. *Oh, how I hate feeling this way!* Escaping Mr. Darcy's presence was as essential as her need to breathe. She turned away from him and immediately was startled by the touch of his hand on her arm. She shuddered. "Pray leave me alone!" Without pausing for even a moment to look back at him, she walked away.

Hours later, Richard found Darcy pacing the floor of his apartment. Darcy halted in his tracks and looked daggers at the older man. "You must allow me to thank you for blurting out our plans to leave Bosley to Miss Bennet."

Richard threw his hands in the air. Cynicism rather than contrition marred his speech, "I take it the course of true love did not run smoothly after I took my leave."

"Miss Bennet was livid, and nothing I could say reversed the damage done in having learned of my plans in such an abrupt manner. She somehow thought that I had been keeping my plans a secret from her. She accused me as much. I do not recall ever seeing her so disappointed."

"It seems a capricious response to me. Are you sure it was not fuelled by those matters of a feminine nature. I have come to expect those periods and a lady's excitability to go hand in hand."

Darcy blew out a long breath. "How on earth you suppose that I would be privy to such a thing is beyond me."

"A man ought to know such things about the woman he plans to marry."

"After the wedding, perhaps." Exasperated with Richard's

cavalier attitude, Darcy threw his hands in the air. "Why am I even discussing such a delicate matter with you, Brutus? The fact is, she is young, and she wants what she wants when she wants it. She has not learned temperance.

"Once she has time to consider it, she will understand that my leaving has nothing to do with any sort of lessened regard for her. I shall call on her before we leave tomorrow." Darcy headed towards the door.

"Where are you off to now?"

"I must see Lord Holland." Darcy could only imagine what his friend would say about his precipitous plans, especially if he learned of the argument with Elizabeth. Lord Holland's words hounded him: *We both know it is solely a matter of time before you do take your leave—rendering the young woman broken-hearted, and when you do, I promise I will be here to pick up the pieces and help mend it back together.*

The next morning, as Elizabeth and her aunt were sitting together in the dining-room, their attention was suddenly drawn to the window by the sound of a carriage. They perceived a chaise and four driving up the lane. Curious as to who would be calling at such an early hour, Elizabeth went to the window to command a better view as well as satisfy both of their curiosities. Elizabeth recognised the vehicle's crest and immediately drew herself away from the window. "Mr. Darcy!" Having now decided that it was better that things had turned out as they had before her heart was truly engaged, he was the last person in the world she wished to see. Heaven forbid that a few well-spoken sentiments on his part might weaken her resolve.

"Pardon me, Lady Vanessa, but I find I am ill equipped to receive guests. Please, make whatever excuse you deem necessary in explaining my absence." She hurried out the door and sped up the stairs.

When Darcy was shown into the room, he greeted her ladyship cordially.

She was equally as cordial. "Mr. Darcy, it is a pleasure seeing you this morning, albeit an unexpected one, but a pleasure nonetheless."

"Your ladyship, as you heard my cousin say, he and I are taking our leave today."

"No doubt you are anxious to arrive in Kent ahead of the upcoming race. Which of your beautiful bays will be running?"

"Perseus will do the honours, your ladyship. He is stabled in Kent" Not intent to engage in small talk a second longer, Darcy cleared his throat. "It is my ardent wish to speak with Miss Bennet before I leave."

Her ladyship threw a cursory glance about the room. "As you can see, sir, Elizabeth is not here."

"Do you suppose she took a walk?" He looked at his watch. "I am familiar with all her favourite lanes. I believe I will seek her out if that does not meet with any objections."

"Actually, sir, Elizabeth is upstairs in her apartment. Furthermore, my niece is aware you are here. She saw you coming. I am afraid she does not wish to see you. Perhaps you had better take your leave. In fact, I insist you do not delay your departure a second longer."

Darcy's astonishment in her attempt to dismiss him could not be repressed. "Pardon me, your ladyship. I simply want to assure her—"

She held up her hand. "Mr. Darcy, let us not quarrel over the matter. The fact is there will *always* be another race."

Chapter 10

Crossed in Love

Not a day had gone by over the past weeks that Lord Holland did not call on Elizabeth and her aunt at Barrington Hall. She attributed it to the less varied society, what with so many of their friends in London for the Season.

"I received a delightful letter from Lucy today," said Elizabeth.

"I should imagine she is enjoying a gay time with this being the height of the Season."

"Indeed. I wonder that you do not go to London as well."

"Why on earth would I do that when everything I want is here?"

Puzzled by his reply, Elizabeth arched her brow. "I should imagine your father would be eager to see you and your mother."

Lord Holland's expression turned sombre. He said nothing.

"Forgive me if I spoke out of turn. It is just that I have yet to meet your father in all the time I have been here. I imagine you must miss each other's company."

"There is a very good reason you have never met his lordship. He is estranged from our family. He prefers to spend all of his time in London, effectively relegating my mother to the country. It is but one of the reasons she throws herself into local society with such alacrity. She misses her place by his side. Alas, it cannot be helped."

Elizabeth, not wishing to intrude on such a delicate matter as he suggested, said no more, and the two walked along in silence.

Lord Holland had no use for his father. What manner of man would banish his wife to the country while he entertained his mistress in Town as if she were the wife? Though he had never met any of them, he was no stranger to accounts of his having *so-called* siblings by at least three different women. What manner of man, indeed. Lord Holland wanted no part of it. His ascension to the earldom could not come soon enough for him in spite of what it would entail.

"When my mother told me that Lady Vanessa and you would not be venturing to Town, I was delighted, albeit a bit puzzled. Do you not enjoy the Season?"

"Actually, I have never had a Season in Town."

"Perhaps that will be rectified next Season."

Elizabeth could not imagine why he would suppose such a thing. Were she in possession of a fortune, she still could not imagine a Season in Town. More and more of late, she could hardly imagine anything other than the nagging pain attributable to Mr. Darcy's leave-taking. As much as she enjoyed Lord Holland's company, it was no substitute for being with Mr. Darcy. At times, she considered she was being most unfair in thinking the way she did. *Lord Holland is a wonderful man—whose greatest failing is that he is not Mr. Darcy,* her traitorous heart whispered. Merely thinking about him, why he had left, and their spat was enough to cast her into a deep pensive attitude.

Lord Holland must have noticed her despair. After a time, he said, "I think Darcy is a fool to have left you as he did."

"He knows his own mind, and he follows his own counsel. I am considering that I might do the same. Despite my commitment to be here in Bosley, I am sorely tempted to return home. I do not know that I am of much service to her ladyship anyway in such a state."

"You might return to Hertfordshire, or you might stay here, but your presence of mind will remain the same. I, for one, should hate to see you take your leave."

Elizabeth rather suspected where their conversation was leading. It would not do. "Lord Holland—"

"I do not believe my feelings for you have been concealed. I would never have treated you with as little consideration as Darcy did. You deserve so much more than his indifference, although I cannot claim any measure of surprise by his defection. It was bound to happen."

Elizabeth said nothing. Lord Holland's speech and his motives as well were exceedingly troubling. On one hand, he had spoken favourably of his own admiration, and on the other, he had disparaged her by insinuating Mr. Darcy—his own friend—incapable of a similar sentimentality.

"Do not be offended, Miss Bennet, if my praise of Darcy is not in every way indicative of my sense of his worth as a good friend. I have known him for many years, and while I have the highest opinion in the world of his honour and his goodness, and I think him everything that is worthy and amiable, he is nothing if not loyal to his family, and he upholds his duty to them above all else. That is not to say he does not hold you in esteem—I would not say that, but it only took the arrival of his cousin to remind him of where his true purposes lie."

"I would never venture to say Mr. Darcy set out to disappoint me."

"He is a fortunate man. He leaves you here, broken-hearted, with no assurance of when he will return, and you make excuses for him."

"Surely I do not mean to offer excuses for Mr. Darcy. As you say, you have known him all your life, and my acquaintance with him is of such short duration. However, his reason for leaving has nothing to do with his loyalty to his family, but rather his passion for his sport."

"I will not argue that is not a great part of it, but you cannot dismiss his obligation to his family out of hand, unless—" The viscount's mouth fell open. "You do not know, do you? But then again how would you? As you said, your acquaintance with him is of short duration."

"What is it you know that you apparently mean for me to know as well, Lord Holland?"

"Darcy's aunt Lady Catherine de Bourgh and her daughter, Anne, reside in Kent."

"He has spoken to me of them more than once. What does his relatives' home in the general vicinity of the racing contest have to do with anything?"

"Darcy's family expects him to marry his cousin Anne. Their engagement, albeit tacit, is of long standing. He has spoken to me of it, and never has he stated his intention not to honour his family's wishes."

Elizabeth did not know how to feel in the wake of Lord Holland's revelation. *Does he speak the truth or does he merely intend to poison me against Mr. Darcy? Was this the reason for the unspoken tension between the gentlemen while Mr. Darcy was here? Did Lord Holland suppose he was protecting me from heartbreak? It will not do. The fact is I am half in love with Mr. Darcy—the one man who has taught my body what it is like to be caressed and my lips what it is like to be kissed. Though I may very well never see him again, I know it will be a very long time before I learn to think otherwise.*

After a long moment of silence, Lord Holland spoke again. "I apologise for having been the one to tell you about Darcy's situation. Pray you are not angry with me—the mere messenger."

"No—not at all," she said.

"Then why are you so quiet all of a sudden?"

Elizabeth knew in her heart that she must leave Bosley. *As much as I enjoy Lord Holland's company, it simply would not be fair to pretend that what Mr. Darcy and I shared during our brief acquaintance meant so little that I would transfer my affections to another over the course of few days, weeks, or even months.*

"I have been pondering the sentiments you expressed earlier—that you admire me. As much as I enjoy spending time in company with you, I do not think it is fair to continue doing so if it gives rise to expectations that I might one day return the feelings you expound."

"You must allow me to be the judge of what is considered fair."

"No, truly my leaving will be better for everyone concerned."

"Your leaving will not serve me, and surely it would disappoint Lady Vanessa. Have you considered how your quitting Bosley will affect her and what it must certainly mean for your future?"

"My life will not be dictated by something that might never come to pass." As Elizabeth was not designed to suffer low spirits over her own misgivings, she added a note of playfulness to her speech. "From everything I have learned about my aunt, she will outlive us all."

Lord Holland chuckled. "I will not argue your point. You know your aunt well." His conciliatory tone gave Elizabeth to know there were no ill feelings as a result of her avowal. As for Lady Vanessa, she might understand—she might not. She might find another person upon whom to heap her benevolence and her fortune, but it did not matter. Elizabeth could not remain in a place that held such bittersweet memories when what she desperately needed was to return to the one place that offered her solace—Longbourn.

Chapter 11

No Humour at Present

Darcy and his aunt Lady Catherine de Bourgh were em-broiled in a heated debate. *Vexing woman!* It took all the control he could muster to remember it was his elderly aunt to whom he was speaking. He took a measured sip of his drink to compose himself. "You cannot be serious about wishing to part with Hercules. He sired five of our family's prize-winning bays."

Her ladyship jutted her chin. "What use must I possibly have for such a possession?"

To Darcy's surprise, her ladyship had invited many of their family to Kent, ostensibly to attend the horse race: his uncle and aunt Lord and Lady Matlock, his young sister, Georgiana, and his cousins Lord Robert and Richard. All of them save his cousin, Anne, Georgiana, and Richard were gathered in Rosings' palatial parlour.

Lord Matlock, who was thought to be napping, sat up and cleared his throat. "What is it that you are saying about Hercules?"

His wife, Lady Ellen, said, "Have you not heard? Lady Catherine is considering selling Hercules to the highest bidder."

"Catherine, how could you? Hercules was our father's favourite possession. You were determined father should give him to you when, by all rights, he should have belonged to me."

"You need not be overly concerned," said Darcy. "I suspect her ladyship has no intention of parting with Hercules at all. This is her thinly disguised attempt to bend me to her will."

Lady Catherine reared her head. "I will not have the two of you speak of me as though I am not in the room. I will have my share of this conversation."

"Is what Darcy says true?"

"I have given him the first right of refusal. He simply has failed to meet my terms."

"How much has he offered you?"

"My terms have nothing to do with money! I have more than enough money. If Darcy wishes to own Hercules, he knows what he must do to satisfy my demands."

"Is this about Anne? My God! Do not tell me you are using your own daughter as a bargaining chip."

"And what if I am? It is not as though Darcy and Anne are not meant for each other. From their cradles, they were destined to be married. It was my sister's as well as my own favourite wish. I am simply making this young man an offer he cannot refuse merely to speed the process along."

"I contend what you are proposing is ludicrous and completely unnecessary. This young man is eight and twenty, and he has yet to choose a bride. There can be but one reason. He knows he must marry your daughter to satisfy his obligation to the family. He is simply biding his time."

"In the meantime, Anne is not getting any younger. Neither am I. I wish to have my grandchildren benefit from my guidance and counsel while I am able to bestow it."

Darcy had heard enough. "Listen to the two of you going on and on about *my* obligations. Your wishes do not obligate me. You and my mother did your part in planning the union. Its execution depends entirely upon others. I do not consider myself engaged—at least not to my cousin."

Lady Catherine's face twisted into a tight grimace. "What on earth is that supposed to mean?"

"You will know when the time is right."

"This is not to be borne! Who is the young lady who has usurped my Anne's rightful place as the next mistress of Pemberley? How is it possible that such a thing could have escaped my knowing?"

Darcy had no intention of satisfying his aunt's curiosity. Darcy swirled the liquor in his fine crystal glass and then took a sip.

Lady Catherine banged her bejewelled mahogany cane against his velvet cushioned chair. "I insist upon being satisfied."

Startled, but far from intimidated, Darcy met his aunt's ferocious stare with one of his own. "I have said all I intend to say for now. I am not at liberty to say more."

"But what about Anne? What about Hercules?"

"If Hercules's fate depends upon my marrying Anne, then I suppose you had better put him down."

Taken aback, her ladyship said, "You speak nonsense, Darcy! What has gotten into you?"

Richard shuffled into the room and drew everyone's attention. "There you are, Fitzwilliam. Your cousin states that he will not marry my Anne, and he does not care about Hercules. He alludes to being engaged to another, but he will not tell me anything about the young woman. What say you about all this?"

Elizabeth needed to speak with her aunt. Now that Lord Holland had stated his intentions towards her in no uncertain terms, she was even more persuaded she would be restless and dissatisfied with her current circumstance. Elizabeth wished for nothing more than to avoid Bosley's society altogether. Longbourn is where she longed to be.

Elizabeth's footsteps echoed quietly as she walked through the corridor of Barrington Hall with sadness she did not think herself capable of when she first arrived in Bosley. Portraits of Barrett family members lined the panelled walls. While Barrington Hall was not her home and did not have the feeling of being home, she had taught herself to appreciate its ostentatious opulence—not because her own tastes had changed, but because this was a reflection of Lady Vanessa's taste. All of this meant something to her aunt. Even the thought that Lady Vanessa had meant for Elizabeth to one day own all of this was not something Elizabeth took for granted. Her late husband, a man that Elizabeth never even knew, had bequeathed his entire fortune to Lady Vanessa, and she had thought to make Elizabeth her sole heir and beneficiary.

Elizabeth found her aunt in the library. She took the seat opposite her. "Might I have a word with you, your ladyship?"

"Of course, you may, my dear. What is on your mind?"

"I have decided to return to Hertfordshire. I am not indifferent to the kindness you have bestowed, but Longbourn is where I need to be, so do not try to dissuade me."

"Elizabeth, my dear, I will not attempt to change your mind. If I know you at all, I know you value the strength of your convictions. You know your own mind. I could not change it, even if I wish. You have no doubt given this a great deal of thought."

"I have."

"Well, I cannot help but consider that this has to do with Mr. Darcy's leave-taking. What a shame that is too. And my dear nephew—surely you know by now how he feels about you."

"I am painfully aware of Lord Holland's sentiments, your ladyship. But I cannot pretend to enjoy similar feelings, nor am I able to hope that I ever will. An alliance between the two of us would subject us both to misery of the acutest kind."

"I will remind you of the terms of my agreement with your father."

Elizabeth listened without speaking as Lady Vanessa continued to make her opinion known; so much for her earlier statement about not attempting to change Elizabeth's mind. However, she was right in saying that any efforts to that effect would be in vain. Elizabeth had thought long and hard on the matter and had formed the conclusion that she could no longer be contented in a place that reminded her so much of Mr. Darcy. She knew if she left now, there was no turning back. She would return to Longbourn with nothing, and her family would be right where they started. She and her sisters would have no connections and no fortune. Any hope her mother held for most advantageous alliances for all her daughters as a consequence of her ladyship's largess would be considerably diminished.

The next morning, Elizabeth stared out the window of her apartment and observed the tranquil countryside for what she was sure would be the last time. Her sister's drawings were removed from the walls, and all her belongings were packed. The room was just as she had found it months prior. She wondered how her father would take the news of her returning to Hertfordshire with no assurances of his sister's intentions. *Surely Papa will not fault me.* She twisted her lower lip and shook her head. *If only the same could be said of my mother.*

Chapter 12

Guilt and Misery

The stifling silence in the carriage forced Darcy to relive his bitter argument with Lady Catherine the day before he took his leave of Kent. Her judgement had been harsh. Her criticisms were severe when she had nothing more on which to base her low opinion of Elizabeth other than Richard's mentioning that the young woman whom Darcy intended to marry was William Collins's cousin.

This is not to be borne, her ladyship had sworn. *Do you know how low an alliance with a woman with such relations would render you in the eyes of the world?* She had encouraged Darcy to call on the Collinses to see for himself just how low that young woman's connections truly were. *My own parson to be cousin to my nephew!* When Darcy could not be prevailed upon to call on the parson and his wife, both strangers to him, her ladyship insisted upon inviting the couple to tea so Darcy might see for himself the manner of people with whom he would be associating should he persist in the notion of offering his hand to Miss Elizabeth Bennet.

Lord Matlock was equally disappointed, but not nearly as disparaging. The morning Darcy left Kent, his lordship had taken him aside to speak man to man. "I have observed a change in you. From what Richard says, this young woman might not enjoy an ideal temperament for a man of your passions."

"Richard is an idiot! What does he know about what is right for me?"

"An *idiot*, as you say, he may be, but in this case, I am inclined to agree with him. It is incomprehensible that you are not planning to attend the upcoming Waltham Mile or even the Ascot races, the most celebrated of them all, preferring instead to return to Bosley to woo this young woman."

"I am no less passionate for the sport, my lord. It is simply that I am more passionate for Miss Bennet. Winning at Richland was a hollow victory. Acquiring Hercules now feels a trivial matter as well. None of this means anything to me without Miss Bennet by my side. I would give it all up if it meant winning her heart."

"Do you not consider you may be behaving too precipitously? You hardly know this young woman."

"When a man meets the woman with whom he is destined to share his life, he knows."

Some hours later, Darcy's carriage arrived at Avondale. His first order of business was speaking with his old friend. Lord Holland stood to greet Darcy when he was shown into the room. "Darcy, you have returned."

"I have, just as I said I would, and I am anxious to rectify any ill feelings."

"Will you join me in a toast to your safe arrival?"

Darcy acquiesced and took a drink. After engaging in talk of trivial matters, Darcy said, "I will allow that you were doing what you felt was needed in admonishing me for my unguarded behaviour with Miss Bennet. No doubt, you care for her. In hindsight, I confess to making mistakes. I might have exercised—"

Lord Holland interrupted. "We both made mistakes."

"That is the reason I came back sooner than I had planned. I made it perfectly clear to my family where my priorities lie. Now I need only call on Miss Bennet at Barrington Hall and attempt to make amends."

"You will not find her at Barrington Hall."

"Did Lady Vanessa and she travel to London for the Season after all?"

"No—her ladyship remains in Bosley."

"Has Miss Bennet returned to Hertfordshire? Did she travel there to visit her family? When did she leave? Have you any idea of when she plans to return?"

"Miss Bennet did indeed return to Hertfordshire, but I do not have any notion of her ever coming back to Bosley."

Darcy found Lord Holland's supposition unsettling. He blew out a frustrated breath.

"You have been gone well over a month. Did you really expect her to wait patiently for your return?"

Darcy knew all along that he had competition from his friend. He had made that perfectly clear prior to Darcy's leave-taking. Darcy also suspected, but never had any proof, that Lord Holland's mother and Lady Barrett were conspiring together for an alliance between Elizabeth and Lord Holland. "Did you not expect her to remain?"

"I have made no secret of my feelings for Miss Bennet, whereas you made no secret that your priorities were elsewhere."

"My purpose in seeing you is not to debate how I might have done things differently."

"It is just as well. The fact is neither of us is with her now. Her leave-taking renders us both losers in winning her heart."

Darcy pondered the options before him. Lord Holland and he were two very different sort of gentlemen, but they need not be adversaries. Leaning forward, he said, "This is a story as old as time. Two men enamoured of the same woman. I do not fault you one bit. Miss Bennet is charming. She is delightful—everything a young woman ought to be. The fact that your mother and aunt desired a match is something that I can hardly fault you with as well. I know what it is like to find oneself in that situation." Darcy stood to take his leave. "As for what happens next, you had better speak for yourself, for I have no intention of losing."

Now back at Longbourn where she truly belonged, Elizabeth endeavoured mightily to resume all her former routines. Elizabeth intended to rectify the one habit she had allowed to falter. She sat at her desk and commenced writing.

> Today marks a week since my return to Longbourn. I would like to say that nothing has changed in all the time I have been away, save Lydia's absence and the ensuing peace that must be expected as a result, but that would not be true. The fact is that much has changed. I have changed.
>
> When I was last at Longbourn, I awakened each day with a sense of loss of my beloved sister that simply would not wane. I returned having come to terms with that loss, but also with a sense of longing. Try as I might to pretend otherwise, there is no point in denying my true feelings. With Lucy and Lord Holland, I might insist upon doing so, but surely not with myself.

When one feels they have nothing to look forward to, one tends to dwell upon the past. Awakening each morning in Bosley and wondering what another day with Mr. Darcy held in store gave me something wonderful to look forward to. His departure dissipated that exhilarating sense of anticipation.

While being back at my beloved Longbourn has helped, I must confess that it is not the balm for my disappointed spirits that I hoped it would be.

Papa has yet to voice dissent over my leaving Bosley and thus ending any chance of reconciliation between Lady Vanessa and him. The same cannot be said of my mother. She is more than disappointed to think that one of her daughters is not a future heiress after all, and that my lot, my sisters' lots, and thereby her lot are as bleak as ever. The one certainty she has as a consequence of my turning away from all that might have been mine is that she will not lift one finger towards finding a husband for me.

How devastated she would be to learn that one of the reasons for my returning was to escape a marriage that was all but arranged by Lady Vanessa. Mama would never understand. I hardly understand it myself. I believe it most unfortunate that I could not be more favourably inclined towards a man who is charming and amiable and whose only failing is he is not Mr. Darcy.

There, I committed the words to paper for all eternity, and now I must forever imagine myself comparing every man I meet to Mr. Darcy and finding the otherwise worthy gentleman wanting.

Meanwhile, Darcy was more than a little annoyed that Lady Barrett had kept him waiting for nearly a half hour. He supposed he deserved her ill treatment. She likely blamed him for Elizabeth's leaving Bosley and based upon what Lord Holland said, Darcy supposed she was correct. He, however, could be just as stubborn as her ladyship. Unlike the last time, he would not be so easily put-off. He would return every day until he gained an audience with her if that is what it took. What he had to say was worth the wait.

Tired of sitting in the same attitude for so long, Darcy stood and walked over to the mantle. There, he espied a miniature of Elizabeth. He pressed his hand to his breast pocket. How he had missed her—longed for her. He missed her teasing smile, her witty repartee, and her lips. He did not wish to miss another day with her. He was still holding her likeness when Lady Vanessa entered the room. Returning the miniature to its proper place, Darcy bowed. "Your ladyship, I thank you for receiving me this morning."

"Mr. Darcy, please have a seat. May I offer you tea?"

Darcy smiled and nodded in acquiescence. Her ladyship busied herself with the preparations and then handed a cup to Darcy. "You are the last person I ever expected to see. What brings you back to Bosley?"

"You will recall my promise to return."

"Indeed. However, I did not expect it would be this soon. You are aware that my niece has returned to Hertfordshire, are you not?"

"Yes, I have come from Avondale. Lord Holland informed me."

"If you have spoken with Lord Holland, then you likely have a full account of what led to my niece's decision to leave. What business can you have with me?"

"Lady Barrett, I know I am the last person you wish to see, but I really must see Miss Bennet again. I require your assistance. It is my ardent wish that you should hear what I have to say."

"I suppose if you are determined, then I shall listen to you, but I make no promise that I can be persuaded to hear anything you have to say with pleasure."

Satisfied that she had granted him an audience, Darcy set aside his cup and began his speech.

Chapter 13

That Kind of Elegance

M ere days after the visit from Mr. Darcy, Lady Vanessa received another member of the illustrious Fitzwilliam family—Lady Catherine de Bourgh. It did not take long before the ladies came to learn how much they had in common, mostly centred on their ideas of forming the perfect alliance for their nephews and the disheartening toll that circumstances had rendered on their hopes and dreams.

Lady Vanessa listened patiently to Lady Catherine before sharing her own thoughts on the matter. "I know exactly how you feel, having suffered a similar situation myself. I know what it is like to have your dreams for an alliance between two young people who seemed destined for one another shattered because one of the two principals is in love with someone else." Lady Vanessa busied herself by refilling her tea. "When did love become a consideration in marriage anyway?"

"It pleases me to hear you speak this way. With the two of us working together towards the greater good of our families, we will be able to thwart my nephew's intentions towards your niece, thus satisfying both our hopes."

"No, Lady Catherine, for that is where you are mistaken. We shall not be working towards a common cause. Unlike you, I know when to lay down the battle-axe."

Hours later, Lady Catherine stewed in her carriage. As irate as she was, she had never been so happy to take her leave of anyone as she was to quit Lady Barrett's company. *The insolence of that woman—who does she suppose she is in inviting me to leave her home? She knows nothing about me to suppose that I would give up my cause so easily as this. I am not in the habit of brokering disappointment. I never surrender!*

Moments later, the carriage ride went from smooth and steady to feeling as though one of the wheels was square. As soon as the carriage drew to a stop, her ladyship banged her cane against the ceiling. Without waiting for assistance, she threw open the door. If Lady Catherine had been paying attention, she would have realised it was not the time to quit the carriage to direct the driver to be quick about resuming the journey. She had no sooner stepped to the ground when the skies above opened up. Poor Lady Catherine was drenched from head to toes in the blink of an eye. She raised a bony fist to the heavens. "This is not to be borne!"

Elizabeth's aunt Mrs. Phillips could hardly wait to share an article of news that had been in circulation in Meryton with her sister, Mrs. Bennet. The housekeeper at Netherfield had received orders to prepare for the arrival of her master who was coming down in a day or two. Mrs. Bennet was quite in the fidgets. Here was a second chance for the determined matriarch to settle one of her daughters on him. Oh, but Mary would never do. As for Elizabeth, her chances of landing him were no better than when he first arrived in Hertfordshire last year. She had failed miserably. How unfortunate that Lydia was away in Brighton with the Forsters. The task of marrying Mr. Bingley now fell firmly on Kitty's shoulders. Though Kitty was not as pretty as Lydia and nowhere near as lively, Mrs. Bennet still supposed that Kitty would admirably do the job of turning Mr. Bingley's head. What other choice was there? Mrs. Bennet was not apt to let a second chance of securing Mr. Bingley as a son-in-law pass her by.

Pangs of distress over her mother's desperation to see all her daughters married pummelled Elizabeth's chest. That same desperation had resulted in Mrs. Bennet sending Jane to a neighbouring estate on horseback on a day that promise a violent storm.

I think I shall never forget that day.

"Mama, I assure you that Mr. Bingley's returning to Hertfordshire has nothing to do with his desire to find a wife. It is more likely he is returning to tend to his estate."

Mrs. Bennet twisted around in her seat to command a full view of her daughter. "How do you know the purpose of his visit, Miss Lizzy?"

"You recall my mentioning his being in Bosley? He said nothing of returning to Netherfield Park for the summer. I suppose some problem has arisen that requires his attention."

"His not mentioning his plan to you tells me that I am correct in supposing that he has no interest in you, and that your sister Kitty stands the better chance of turning his head than you!"

Elizabeth was satisfied to escape her mother's scheme. *What a shame a man cannot visit his own home without creating such excitement and speculation.* With all this talk of Mr. Bingley returning to Hertfordshire, Elizabeth's thoughts naturally tended to his friend Mr. Darcy. She knew there was little chance of him joining the Netherfield party. As much as Elizabeth did not want to admit it, following the news of the horse races had become her secret passion. *If I know anything at all about Mr. Darcy, he is preparing for the Ascot races.*

Elizabeth wondered how it would be seeing Mr. Bingley again after their time together in Bosley. She prayed his sister did not plan to join him, for she could well imagine herself being the object of quite a bit of derision owing to her disappointed hopes. Though Elizabeth had no proof, she well imagined that Caroline Bingley had played a part in dampening Mr. Darcy's admiration for her. *How she must be congratulating herself on her triumph.*

Elizabeth's greatest solace imaginable in once again being in proximity to the Bingleys was her knowledge that Caroline's hopes for an alliance with Mr. Darcy would never be realised. Elizabeth had by now convinced herself that Mr. Darcy intended to honour his family's wishes and marry his cousin Miss Anne de Bourgh.

Elizabeth recalled the look on his face as he stood outside his carriage at Barrington Hall—the last time she ever saw him when she had refused to receive him. She had removed herself from his vantage point in the window just in time to prevent his seeing her. He just stood there for a long while as if silently commanding that she come out and see him before finally boarding his carriage and taking his leave.

She did not know at the time that he was engaged, even if only tacitly, to his cousin in Kent. She was simply angry and disappointed, in herself more than anything else, for allowing herself to become attached to him. Silent recriminations haunted her. If she had seen him, would it have made a difference? Would he have come back as he had said he would? Would he have gone against his family's wishes and offered for her? *What is the point in conjecture?*

Two days later, Kitty, who had been sitting in the window seat staring out, was suddenly aroused. "A gentleman is coming!"

"Is it Mr. Bingley? Mama will be disappointed to have missed him."

"It is not Mr. Bingley. I have never laid eyes on him before. He is a tall, proud looking man."

Eager to satisfy her own curiosity, Elizabeth hurried to the window and peered outside. Her heart slammed against her chest, and she quickly reclaimed her seat. She placed her hand over her bosom to steady her breathing. *It is Mr. Darcy!*

Darcy paced the floor in the hallway outside the library waiting to be received by the gentleman of the manor house. Whatever were his thoughts on the recognition of the inferiority of Elizabeth's circumstances in comparison to his own, Darcy would not be deterred. The weeks he had spent with her in Bosley were the most satisfying in all his life. No woman had ever bewitched him so. The time away from her had been a torment. He *would* see her again.

Pray she does not cling to her disappointment over what she must have perceived as my ill treatment of her.

Finally, the housekeeper emerged from the room and stepped aside to allow him to pass. "The master will see you now, sir."

The silver-haired patriarch stood when Darcy entered the room. Darcy bowed slightly. "Good morning, sir. Thank you for agreeing to see me."

The older gentleman arched his bushy brow. "It is a fine morning indeed. To whom do I have the pleasure of welcoming to my home?"

"I am Fitzwilliam Darcy of Pemberley and Derbyshire."

"Derbyshire—that is quite a distance from Hertfordshire, but I do not need to tell you that." He signalled Darcy to take a seat. "How might I serve you?"

"I have come from Bosley. I have a letter from Lady Barrett." Darcy handed the letter to Mr. Bennet. Mr. Bennet accepted the missive, opened the elegant seal, and perused its contents. He shifted his gaze from the letter to Mr. Darcy with regularity. Of course, Darcy had no idea what Lady Barrett had written, but he hoped he had been able to persuade her lady-ship that his intentions towards Elizabeth were honourable. She had given him no assurances of his success or lack thereof and had only asked that he deliver the letter to Mr. Bennet upon his arrival in Hertfordshire. Darcy had placed a great deal of trust in Lady Barrett's hands—an unprecedented act for a man who always relied upon his own counsel.

Few words had been spoken between Darcy and Mr. Bennet. When Mr. Darcy was gone, Mr. Bennet sought out his wife to apprise her of the events of the morning. Upon being informed the lady of the manor had ventured to town while he was receiving his guest, Mr. Bennet was obliged to await her return. All the while, he amused himself with the notion of heightening his wife's aggravation by keeping her in suspense as long as possible.

When finally the housekeeper informed him of his wife's return, he found her in the parlour with Elizabeth, Mary, and Kitty. He cleared his throat, thus summoning everyone's attention. "I hope, my dear, that you have ordered a good dinner today, for we are to expect an addition to our family party."

"Who do you mean, Mr. Bennet? I know of nobody that is coming, I am sure, unless Maria Lucas should happen to call in—and I hope my dinners are good enough for her. I do not believe she often sees such at home."

The elderly gentleman was not one to move quickly to the point when an opportunity to excite his wife's spirits presented itself. "The person of whom I speak is a gentleman and a stranger—to some of us, at least."

Mrs. Bennet's eyes sparkled. "A gentleman and a stranger! It is Mr. Bingley, I am sure! But why should you consider him a stranger? True, it has been many months since he left Netherfield. He did promise to take a family dinner with us when he returned, but he certainly is no stranger. Well, I am sure I shall be extremely glad to see Mr. Bingley. But—good Lord! How unlucky! There is not a bit of fish to be got today. Kitty, ring the bell; I must speak to Hill this moment."

"It is not Mr. Bingley," said her husband.

"Who is it then? Is it the young man whom Hill said called on you earlier? He got away before any of us could be introduced." Mrs. Bennet commenced attacking her husband in various ways—with barefaced questions, ingenious suppositions, and distant surmises, but he eluded the skill of them all.

At length, he put an end to his teasing. He peered over his glasses and directed his eyes towards his favourite daughter. "I believe Lizzy is the only one of us in the position to answer your questions justly." He tucked his arms behind his back. "My dear Lizzy, I shall leave you to it."

As soon as he was gone, Mrs. Bennet and the girls swarmed Elizabeth with questions. Elizabeth ventured to answer them as best she could while trying to reveal as little as possible. She had weightier matters to occupy her thoughts, and she could hardly wait until she was alone to think.

Her astonishment at his coming to Hertfordshire—to Longbourn—and voluntarily seeking her again was almost unequal to anything she had known since first making his acquaintance. To come so far after she had treated him so callously by refusing to see him when he called on her at Barrington before taking his leave to Kent must surely mean that he was not as angry with her as she had taught herself to believe. But she would not be secure. *Let me first see how he behaves. Then I shall know what to expect.*

Shortly after Mr. Darcy had arrived and the introductions were made, he found himself seated at the dinner table with Elizabeth and her family. Earlier, Mrs. Bennet had made enough inquiries to ascertain that the gentleman had ten thousand pounds a year. Her anxiety increased one-hundred fold. Though she always kept a very good table, she did not think anything less than two courses could be good enough to satisfy the appetite and pride of such a man. With such short notice, Mrs. Bennet was more than a little annoyed that she had not the time to plan a proper dinner party, one that included the finest families of her acquaintance, for her esteemed guest. Alas, it was to be a small family dinner. Not even her own sister could be prevailed upon to attend on such short notice, owing to prior commitments.

For that, Elizabeth was exceedingly grateful. It would not do for Mr. Darcy's first meeting with her Hertfordshire relations to be marred by her aunt's vulgarity. Elizabeth worried enough over what her mother might do and say.

"It was kind of you to seek our society, Mr. Darcy. It is such an honour," said Mrs. Bennet. "However, where is Mr. Bingley? How delighted we were when he let Netherfield Park after it had stood empty for so very long. Does he ever intend to return, or does he have a notion of ending his lease? Surely if he plans never to return, he ought to give it up. Is that the purpose in your coming to Hertfordshire, sir? Do you intend to procure the estate for your own purposes?"

Her husband said, "Mrs. Bennet, you must allow the young man a moment to answer one question at a time."

"Nonsense, Mr. Bennet. The neighbourhood was quite disappointed when Mr. Bingley left and without choosing a future bride from amongst any of the single young ladies. Pray tell, Mr. Darcy, does Mr. Bingley remain single?"

"When last we spoke, he was single, madam."

Elizabeth feared she would roll under the table should the question of Mr. Darcy's marital plans arise? Fortunately, her mother's attention was drawn away when Kitty, whom she had purposely seated directly beside the gentleman, began coughing incessantly.

"For heaven's sake, Kitty! Do you know no better than to create such a commotion in the presence of our distinguished guest?" She returned her attention to Mr. Darcy. "I do hope the meal is to your liking, sir, although I suppose you must have two or three French cooks at least."

Darcy said that he did not, and he further complimented her on the excellent meal. A very fine meal it was: venison, partridges, a fat haunch as well as the finest soup to be had— fifty times better than what he would have been served at Lady

Lucas's table. His commendations pleased Mrs. Bennet immensely, and soon she began to speak on other topics to garner his approbation.

Having exhausted several awkward topics, Mrs. Bennet began praising her daughter Kitty. "All my daughters are accomplished young ladies and none more than my Kitty. She paints screens, she draws exceedingly well, and she has a thorough command of the modern languages."

Elizabeth nearly laughed aloud. *Can this be my younger sister?* Elizabeth had to turn her face to hide her amusement. When Mrs. Bennet extolled Kitty's accomplishments on the pianoforte, even poor Mary's countenance clouded with bewilderment. Elizabeth, well aware that the designs her mother had intended for Mr. Bingley and Kitty were now being directed to Mr. Darcy and Kitty, began to feel sorry he had come at all.

Elizabeth said as little to the gentleman as civility would allow, preferring instead to study his reactions to those he no doubt considered beneath him in consequence. When she could, she stole a glance at her father, but all she detected was his amusement in watching Mr. Darcy looking embarrassed and ill at ease while endeavouring to survive the onslaught of a very determined matchmaking mamma.

Mr. Darcy resumed his same attitude from dinner to the parlour. Elizabeth had always known he could be brooding, but never had she seen him so quiet, so taciturn in company. With his friends in Bosley, he was always amicable. He behaved equally agreeable with Lady Vanessa who did not hide the fact that she would rather he were Lord Holland. *But that must be his way—exceedingly agreeable amongst those whom he considers his equals. I made it clear to him that the other members of my family were not part of the fashionable society, did I not? How did he expect them to be? Why come at all if he meant to be silent and taciturn?*

When it was time for the guest to take his leave, Mr. Bennet suggested that Elizabeth see the gentleman out. She was more than happy to be of service. As soon as they were alone, Eliza-

beth crossed her arms and commenced her long-awaited inter-
rogation. "What is the purpose in your being here, sir?"

"I think you know the reason I am here."

"I think in such cases as this, I would rather not suppose
anything, sir."

"I came to see you. I had to see you. Being apart from you
for all these weeks has been a torment."

"So, spending time with me once again meets with your
busy schedule, Mr. Darcy?"

Darcy clasped his hands behind his back. Clearly, she did
not intend to make this easy for him, despite his having suffered
the one of the most trying evenings of his adult life. He stood
straight and tall. "I admit I might have handled matters better
as regarded my abrupt departure from Bosley. If I had it to do
over, I would have done things differently. I wager you would
say the same."

"Perhaps a bit of temperance might have been in order, but
I shall not apologise for feeling as I did."

"Nor do I expect you to." Darcy looked around to discern if
anyone else was about. Seeing no one, he took Elizabeth by the
hand and led her away from the vantage point of the windows.
He brushed a kiss across her knuckles. Still holding her hand, he
said, "There is much I wish to say to you. I recall you mentioning Oakham Mount when we were together in Bosley. I have
made inquiries on how I might find the place. Meet me there in
the morning."

"How do I know you will not steal away in the middle of
the night on some urgent matter pertaining to your sport?"

His face registered his astonishment. "Miss Bennet, you are
not being fair. I told you I would return to Bosley. You chose not
to wait for me."

"Did you really expect me to stay in Bosley when everything about the place held memories of you?"

Darcy hushed Elizabeth with a touch of his finger upon her
lips. "I am here now. You and I shall create new memories."

Chapter 14

What They Ought to Be

As much as Elizabeth enjoyed the fresh morning air as well as Mr. Darcy's companionship, if she would but admit it, his taciturn manner was a cause for discomfort. She surmised some conversation was in order. After many pauses and many trials of various subjects, she ventured upon one that would surely satisfy her curiosity over his being there.

"Did Lord Holland tell you that I had returned to Hertford-shire?"

"Actually, he and I spoke on a number of subjects concerning you."

"Oh?"

"You need not feel embarrassed. I could no more be angry with him for his ardent admiration of you than I could be angry with myself. We share similar tastes."

"I will allow that he and I discussed a great many things concerning you, as well."

"No doubt."

"Have you not the slightest bit of curiosity about what we discussed?"

"You are determined to tell me, so I am obliged to listen."

"Well, I normally would not say anything at all, but you are here, and I feel it a matter that truly must be discussed if we are to reclaim our prior standing as friends."

"I should like to think we were more than just friends." Darcy reached for Elizabeth's hand, but she pulled away. "Pray tell me what did Lord Holland say that you want to discuss with me?"

"He said you were engaged to be married—to your cousin Miss Anne de Bourgh. Of course, he did say it was a tacit engagement and one that your family desired. He persuaded me that your purpose in leaving Bosley was to honour your family's expectation. I considered all he said in conjunction with your cousin's arrival and your subsequent hasty departure. I was compelled to attribute irrefutable truth to Lord Holland's pronouncement."

"It is not true. I am not engaged to my cousin. I never have been, and I never will be. Lord Holland should not have told you such a falsehood. He knows where my heart lies."

"How could he possibly know the workings of another person's heart?"

"Believe me when I say, he knows. Surely you know it as well. His sole purpose in telling you about Anne was because he wanted you to doubt my constancy. It seems he accomplished his mission."

"Mr. Darcy, if I have been given to doubt your constancy, it has very little to do what Lord Holland told me."

"Then what other reason would you possibly have?"

"You ... you led me to believe I was important to you ... that you were someone I could depend on—when depending upon another was the last thing I ever wished for myself. You led me to believe I could trust you, but then you left so hastily with vague assurances that you would return. What was I to think?"

"You *can* trust me. I said I would return as soon as my business was settled, and I did. In fact, I returned even sooner than I had planned. I had to see you. I could no longer bear the thought of us being apart. When I returned to find you gone, I came here as soon as arrangements could be made with Bingley to send orders to his housekeeper at Netherfield to prepare for my arrival.

"Now that I am here, I do not intend to waste another minute discussing Lord Holland and what his purposes were or my family's expectations. All that means nothing to me, and it should matter even less to you.

"I will allow that I have made mistakes and suffered in your opinion because of it, but I will make things right again. I promise."

Elizabeth thought long on the matter of whether or not to be truly happy about Mr. Darcy's return. She had to admit that she was quite unhappy during the time they were apart. That emptiness she felt subsequent to his leave-taking was replaced merely by his smile when they greeted each other the evening before. *Still, he made it abundantly clear that matters of business—nay, sport were of utmost importance to him.*

"I am actually surprised that you have come, Mr. Darcy. Does your being here mean that one of your horses is not racing in Ascot?"

Darcy's countenance spoke to his amazement that she was knowledgeable of such a thing.

"I would be lying if I said I have not been following the sport since I was introduced to it in Bosley."

"I am competing in Ascot. However, that does not mean I will be there. I am exactly where I need to be. My cousin Richard will oversee my interests."

"Ah, your cousin Richard."

"You say that as though you do not approve of him."

"He is perfectly amiable, but I suspect he took a little too much pleasure in being the one to inform Lady Vanessa and me of your plans to leave Bosley in the manner in which he did."

"Well, he was doing my aunt Lady Catherine de Bourgh's bidding. I believe that once you get better acquainted with him, you will like him very much."

"You presume a great deal to suppose he and I will ever lay eyes on each other again."

"What else can I do? To suppose the two of you will never meet again would be to admit that I have failed miserably in my quest to win your heart. *That,* I assure you, is unacceptable."

"Mr. Darcy, may I speak frankly?"

"Please do."

"First, I will admit to being flattered by your attention. What is more, I have missed spending time with you. I did not enjoy feeling as I did during the time we were apart. But that is the thing; I did not like feeling that way. Rather than risk feeling that way again, I would rather feel nothing at all."

"Surely you do not mean what you are saying."

"I am rather certain I do."

Darcy captured her hand in his. "I know what this is about. You are afraid." Gently massaging her palm, he said, "I know I disappointed you by my precipitous leave-taking from Bosley. At the time, I supposed I had no other choice. However, I quickly came to know that my reasons for leaving so abruptly were paltry and inconsequential. Had I to do it again, my choice would be different."

Elizabeth neither confirmed nor denied the veracity of his sentiments. Instead, she pulled her hand away from his tender grasp and put a bit of distance between them.

Darcy remained in place and clutched his hands behind his back. However, he would not be dissuaded from his purpose. "It is understandable that you are reluctant to give away your heart. You fear feeling again as you did when you lost your sister. Believe me, I understand. I liken your feelings to those I suffered when I lost my mother at such a young age. I closed myself off from the world, knowing that in so doing, I might never suffer the heartrending pain of loss again. But life does not work that way. I had to learn to relinquish my inhibitions and dare to live life to its fullest. I ask that you do the same."

"You will admit then that there is something to be said about protecting oneself."

"Yes, but you do not need to protect yourself from me. I would never do anything to hurt you. I cannot swear that I will never disappoint you again, for I am sure I most certainly will. Neither of us is perfect. As long as we live and embrace life to its fullest, we shall be subjected to those human frailties that render disillusionment. Such is the joy in living, giving something of ourselves to the unpredictable, the uncertainty."

"Mr. Darcy, I—"

Darcy quickly approached her and brushed his thumb across her lower lip. "Miss Bennet, I cannot tell you how much I missed you while I was away from Bosley—away from you." By now, they were standing rather close. He leaned in, even as he sensed her pulling away.

His delicate touch took her breath away. She felt the heat spread over her body as she pressed her hands to his chest. "This is all happening too fast."

"I know it might seem that way, but for me, this has been too long in coming." She had not rejected him, and that alone was encouraging enough. His mood lightened, he held up his hands in mock surrender. "However, I am a patient man."

This portrait of him brought an amused smile to Elizabeth's face.

"What? It is true, and I shall prove it to you."

"We shall see, Mr. Darcy." Elizabeth tore her eyes away from his and gazed at the mid-morning sky. "It is getting late. My family will wonder what is keeping me."

"May I see you back to the village?"

"I would much prefer to walk, and you have your carriage."

"Then I will walk with you."

"I do not think—"

Before she knew what she was about, Mr. Darcy claimed her in his arms. He silenced her protest with a brush of his lips atop the tip of her nose. Elizabeth sucked in a quick breath and placed her hand atop her bosom, willing her heart to be still. She could hardly say no after that.

Upon their arrival, Darcy and Elizabeth entered the house, and right away she could tell something was amiss—as though a gloomy cloud hovered all about. The housekeeper, usually pleasant and amiable, bore a grave and serious expression. From the hallway, Darcy and Elizabeth could hear Mrs. Bennet's unsettling lamentations.

"What shall become of my poor, poor Lydia?"

Elizabeth grabbed the housekeeper's arm, but before she could muster a sound, the colonel from the brigade that had decamped to Brighton, Colonel Forster, sped past Darcy and her on his way out the door in such haste he barely acknowledged they were standing there.

"What on earth is happening?" Elizabeth raced into the parlour. "Mama, pray what has happened that has upset you so? Colonel Forster passed us in the hallway." She drew a deep breath. "This has to do with Lydia! Pray she has met with no harm."

Mary said, "It is the worst possible thing you could ever imagine."

Chills poured over Elizabeth's body causing her to tremble. "Lydia—dead!"

"No—it is even worse. Lydia has run away! She has thrown herself into the power of Mr. Wickham."

It took more than a moment for Elizabeth to register what Mary had said. At length, she managed to breathe. *My sister is not dead. My sister is alive. Is she safe? She has run away with the lieutenant. Poor Lydia—she has no money, no connections—absolutely nothing that would tempt him to behave honourably should he choose not to. Is that a fate worse than death?*

A strong hand on her shoulder recalled her to the present. She looked at Darcy, who was seated next to her, for a long while as time stood still amidst the wailings of her mother and as the preaching by her sister Mary faded into the background. She heard him saying, in a tone of gentleness and commiseration, "I am so sorry. You are understandably upset, but you must calm yourself. A glass of wine ... shall I get you one?"

"No, I thank you," she replied, endeavouring to recover her composure. "I am quite well." She was anything but. Hot tears threatened to burst from her eyes. Darcy, in wretched suspense, could only say something indistinctly of his concern and observe her in compassionate silence.

Elizabeth wrung her hands. She could hardly summon the strength to utter the words. "Lydia is lost forever."

Darcy was fixed in astonishment. "I am grieved indeed." He directed his next inquiry to Mary. "But is it certain—absolutely certain?"

"Oh, yes! They left Brighton together on Sunday night and were traced almost to London, but not beyond. They are certainly not gone to Scotland." Mary pushed her glasses against her face and attempted to reclaim her usual solemn composure. "This is a very thoughtless act on my sister's part, and one that has brought shame upon us all."

"And what is being done? What is being attempted to recover her?"

"My father is preparing to go to London as we speak, where he shall beg my uncle's immediate assistance. But nothing can be done. I know very well that nothing can be done. How are they even to be discovered? I have not the smallest hope. This situation is in every way horrible!"

Darcy made no answer. He seemed scarcely to hear her. He walked up and down the room in earnest meditation, his brow contracted, and his air gloomy. Elizabeth soon observed this and instantly understood it. Her power was sinking. Everything must sink under such a proof of family weakness and such an assurance of the deepest disgrace. She could neither wonder nor condemn, for what decent person would wish to associate with the Bennets ever again?

Now relatively composed, Elizabeth stood and faced Mr. Darcy. "I suppose you have long desired to take your leave."

"No, how can you say such a thing?"

"Sir, this truly is a private matter—one that cannot possibly be of any concern to you. I begin to consider that your leaving will be for the best. This cannot be very pleasant for you."

"I cannot leave you in such a state."

"No, I thank you," she said, endeavouring to recover herself. "However, you need not worry over me."

"Perhaps I might be of assistance to your family."

"There is nothing that you can do that is not being done. My father and my uncle will do all they can to discover them." Instilling her voice with resolve, Elizabeth said, "Mr. Darcy, I really must attend my mother and sisters. Shall I see you to the door?"

Darcy reluctantly conceded the request. Assuring her that he would see himself out, he again expressed his sorrow for her distress, wished it a happier conclusion than there was at present reason to hope, and with a serious, parting look, went away.

As he quitted the room, Elizabeth felt how improbable it was that they should ever see each other again. She threw a retrospective glance over the whole of their acquaintance, so full of contradictions and varieties, and painfully rejoiced in its termination. She was certain that her family was ruined, owing to this wretched business. She did not dare entertain the hope that the gentleman who had absconded with her sister would marry the poor girl.

I recall Mr. Darcy having insinuated unpleasant things about Mr. Wickham's character when I first mentioned the gentleman's name in Bosley. However, he never provided any specifics, and I surely did not ask. Had I done more to learn about Mr. Wickham's character, could I have prevented this tragedy?

The more she considered it, the more she knew that she might have done nothing to prevent it. Never once did she consider that someone as young and naïve as Lydia could have attracted the officer's notice. But now it was all too natural. For such an attachment as this, Lydia certainly had sufficient charms. Though Elizabeth did not suppose Lydia to be deliberately engaging in an elopement without the intention of marriage, she had no difficulty in believing that neither her virtue nor her understanding would preserve her from becoming an easy prey.

Before leaving for Bosley, Elizabeth had never perceived, while the regiment was in Hertfordshire, that Lydia had any partiality for Mr. Wickham, but she was convinced that Lydia wanted only encouragement to attach herself to anybody. *Sometimes one officer, sometimes another, had been her favourite, as their attentions raised them in her opinion. Her affections had continually been fluctuating but never without an object.* Now the mischief of neglect and mistaken indulgence towards such a girl by her parents had rendered them all unsuitable as wives of any decent gentleman. How acutely she had felt it as she had watched Mr. Darcy take his leave.

Chapter 15

Stronger Than Virtue

Over a week later, surrounded by filth, Darcy stood outside the door and pounded. His nemesis could be heard barking orders before the door slowly crept opened. "Well, well, what do we have here? *The* Fitzwilliam Darcy of Pemberley and Derbyshire. What on earth brings you to this part of Town?" He huffed. "No doubt it will take years for you to rid yourself of the stench."

Pursuing his former friend had taken far longer than he would have wished: tiresome questioning of some of the town's vilest creatures and even bribery, but he had finally done it. *Now I find myself in the hallway of this filthy rat hole.*

George Wickham's hair was tussled, and his shirt hung loosely from his trousers. Heaven knows what Darcy had interrupted. Wickham stepped aside. "Well, do not just stand there. Come in and have a seat." Directing Darcy to a cluttered wooden chair, Wickham swept his coat and other belongings to the floor. Waving his hand, he said, "Welcome to my humble abode—such that it is. I would offer you a drink," he waved the half-empty decanter, "but I am rather low in spirits."

Darcy clutched his hat tightly. "This is not a social call."

"I do not suppose it is—especially in view of the way we parted in Ramsgate." He took a swig from the bottle, and then wiped his mouth on his sleeve. "How is your lovely sister?"

"You reprobate! How dare you mention my sister?"

From the moment he had heard of the terrible fate visited upon Elizabeth's family, this sorry state of affairs had caused Darcy to think about a circumstance that he wished to forget: his entire sordid history with Wickham and what it nearly had cost him.

Wickham was the son of a very respectable man, the elder Mr. Darcy's steward. Owing to the elder Mr. Wickham's good conduct in the discharge of his duties, the late Mr. Darcy liberally bestowed his kindness on George Wickham, who was his godson. He supported him at school and afterwards at Cambridge. He was not only fond of the young man, whose manner was always engaging, but he also had the highest opinion of him. Hoping the church would be his profession, the late Mr. Darcy intended to provide for him in that. Darcy, himself, thought of Wickham in a very different manner. The vicious propensities—the want of principle—which he was careful to guard from the knowledge of his benefactor, could not escape the observation of a young man of nearly the same age with himself, and who had opportunities of seeing him in unguarded moments.

The elder Mr. Darcy's attachment to Mr. Wickham was so steady that in his will he particularly recommended to his son to promote Wickham's advancement in the best manner that his profession might allow. If Wickham took orders, the late Mr. Darcy desired that a valuable family living might be his as soon as it became vacant. There was also a legacy of one thousand pounds. Within half a year from these events, Mr. Wickham wrote and informed Darcy that he much preferred cash in lieu of the living. He had some intention of studying law, and the interest of one thousand pounds was insufficient to support his desired way of life.

Wishing more than believing him to be sincere, Darcy readily acceded to Wickham's proposal. Knowing that Wickham ought not to be a clergyman, the business was therefore soon settled, and Wickham resigned all claim to assistance in the church were it possible that he could ever be in a situation to receive it. He accepted in return three thousand pounds. All connection between the two seemed now dissolved, for Darcy thought too ill of Wickham to invite him to Pemberley, or admit his society in Town.

When the living became available, Wickham returned to see Darcy. He had found the law a most unprofitable study. He was subsequently resolved on being ordained if Darcy would present him to the living in question, just as the elder Mr. Darcy had intended. When Darcy refused to comply with this petition, Wickham's resentment was in proportion to the distress of his circumstances. He violently reproached Darcy and vowed his revenge.

Wickham smirked. "How did you find me?"

"I uncovered every rock I could until I finally sought your partner in the attempted ruin of my sister."

Darcy did not need to be more specific, for Wickham could have suffered no doubt over whom Darcy was speaking. After their altercation at Pemberley, every appearance of acquaintance between the two men was dropped until last summer when he painfully obtruded on Darcy's notice with Darcy's young sister, Georgiana, in his sights. About a year prior, she had been taken from school and an establishment formed for her in London. Last summer she went with the lady, a Mrs. Younge, who presided over it, to Ramsgate. Thither also went Mr. Wickham, undoubtedly by design, for there proved to have been a prior acquaintance between him and Mrs. Younge, in whose character Darcy had been most unhappily deceived.

By her connivance and aid, Wickham was able to recommend himself to Georgiana, whose affectionate heart retained a strong impression of his kindness to her as a child. He persuaded her to believe herself in love and to consent to an elopement. She was then but fifteen, which must be her excuse. Darcy joined them unexpectedly a day or two before the intended elopement, and then Georgiana, unable to support the idea of grieving and offending a brother whom she almost looked up to as a father, acknowledged the whole to him. Wickham's chief object was unquestionably young Miss Darcy's fortune of thirty thousand pounds. Darcy always supposed that Wickham's hope of retaliation was a strong inducement as well.

Had Darcy not thwarted Wickham's scheme, the latter's revenge would have been complete indeed.

"Come now, Darcy. You and I were the best of friends at one time."

A young woman poked her head out the door of the adjacent room. "I shall be out to receive our guest as soon as can be."

"Stay where you are, Lydia." He shook his head and rolled his eyes. "You little fool," he mumbled. Aiming his ire straight back at Darcy, Wickham said, "My business does not concern you."

Darcy shook his head. "That is where you are mistaken. My purpose in being here has everything to do with Miss Bennet."

Still gripping his bottle in his hand, Wickham crossed one arm over the other. "Here you are again, riding in on your white horse to rescue another damsel in distress. It is a shame that you arrived in Ramsgate when you did. I might well have been your brother by now, and we surely would not be standing around in this wretched place."

Lydia poked her head into the room again. "Whatever do you mean in saying you might have been his brother? Who is this tall, proud man? Whoever you are, sir, am I correct in hearing that your sister had designs on *my* Wickham? La! Is she prettier than I am?" She huffed. "Of course she could not possibly be, for my Wickham says that I am the loveliest woman in all of England." She looked at him with her eyes full of lust. "Is that not what you whisper to me every time we—" Gasping, she slapped her hand over her mouth. "Heavens, I ought not to have said a word about any of that."

The look both men bestowed spoke louder than words and prompted Lydia to draw her head back in her room.

"I fail to comprehend what interest you might possibly hold in the likes of her? How are you even aware of whom she is?"

"I am under no obligation to divulge any of that information to you. Suffice it to say the young woman's family is devastated."

Mindless of her dishevelled attire and unkempt hair, Lydia pranced into the room. "Why on earth would my family be devastated by my marrying the handsomest, most amiable man in the world, and an officer no less?" She clasped both hands to her face to contain her exuberance. "The youngest daughter married before the eldest! Who should have imagined such a thing? Mind you, I did write to my dear friend Harriet providing her the strongest hint of our intentions. She was to tell Sally to mend a great slit in my worked muslin gown before they are packed up—"

Wickham marched towards her, forcing her to trace her steps backwards. "I do not wish to hear another word from you. Do I make myself clear?" She nodded and retreated into the room. He grabbed the knob and slammed the door. "Do not force me to lock this door! The next time, I will!"

Darcy ran his fingers through his hair. *Why am I wasting my time on a silly young girl so deficit of sense and feeling as to consent to live with a man on terms other than marriage? The fact that she has chosen to follow Wickham down this scandalous path of shame makes her even more pitiable.* Wishing to be done with the two of them as soon as possible, Darcy knew there was only one route to a speedy resolution—the one that led straight to Gretna Green.

A knock at the door summoned their attention. Wickham sauntered over to the door and pulled it open. "Who in hell is this?" he barked, glaring over his shoulder at Darcy.

Darcy approached and greeted the elderly woman. "Mrs. Shaw, thank you for coming. I am sorry to ask you to do this and even more sorry to subject you to such conditions, but there is no other way. You will find the young woman in the adjacent room."

Lydia, who had not been deterred from listening to the goings-on outside her door, bounced into the room again. "La! Have we another caller? Two callers in one morning, I shall go distracted."

"Quiet, Lydia!" Wickham's heightened colour evidenced his exhausted patience. "Go back inside until I say it is acceptable for you to come out."

In a manner reminiscent of a petulant child, Lydia stomped her foot and crossed her arms. "Am I not the mistress of my home? Is it not my privilege to receive our guests?"

Glowering, Wickham lunged towards her, but Lydia scuttled off in a flash. Mrs. Shaw trailed behind her. He rubbed his hand over his face and blew out a sharp breath. All but dropping to his knees, Wickham said, "Darcy, take her away, and take that old woman with you. I assume that is her purpose in being here."

"It will not be as simple as that. The young woman is ruined. What is more, her entire family risks ruin because of your debauchery. There is but one way to rectify the situation. You must marry her."

"Marry her?" Wickham snorted. "You know as well as anyone that my habits of taste require that I marry a woman of means. Why would I marry this silly girl? You and I both know she is not the first to throw herself at me. I dare say she will not be the last."

"Silence, Wickham! You *will* marry her, and before you protest further, you ought to know that while I was turning over every rock to find you, I had my man conduct a thorough inquiry on your spending habits in Meryton and Brighton. It seems you incurred significant debts. You can have no doubt who now holds the notes. So, unless you fancy a good long stint in prison owing to your inability to pay your sizeable debts, you will marry the girl."

Wickham raked his fingers through his hair and then placed his hand about his waist. "How am I to support a wife, a home, and, heaven forbid, children? Do you mean to grant me the living that ought to have been mine all along?"

Darcy laughed aloud. "Leave it, Wickham! How you mean to support yourself is none of my concern." Darcy considered it was Elizabeth's sister he was subjecting to such a fate. "Although you were amply compensated in the past in lieu of the living, I am not unreasonable. I am willing to discuss arrangements to set you and your bride on a steady path."

A half hour later, Darcy pushed himself away from the rickety wooden table where Wickham and he had hammered out the scheme. His purse was destined to be lighter by nearly ten thousand pounds by the time it was all done, but it was worth it. The worst Elizabeth's family need endure was the embarrassment of the youngest daughter's elopement to Gretna Green, which they must surely consider a blessing in view of the alternative.

"Gather your belongings, Wickham. You are coming with me."

"Why should I leave? Is that not the purpose of your bringing that old woman around—that she might escort Lydia to her relatives in Cheapside or even Grosvenor Square to remain until our travel arrangements can be made?"

Darcy huffed. "Grosvenor Square? Do not be absurd! Besides, the young woman's family knows nothing of any of this. The only thing they will know is that the two of you were married in Gretna Green, just as she had informed her friend. You shall make whatever excuse you wish in explaining your delay in returning to England.

"Mrs. Shaw will remain here with Miss Bennet, and you shall come with me. I have no intention of letting you out of my sight until the two of you exchange wedding vows, at which point, I hope never to see you again."

Deep in thought in the carriage en route to his Grosvenor Square townhouse, Darcy would not be entirely satisfied with the way things unfolded. Ever since he first learned of what happened in Brighton, he was consumed with a single burning question.

He looked at his companion with disgust. "You care nothing about that young woman, or else you would not have treated her as little more than a whore. She has no fortune, nothing to recommend her. Why did you single her out for your malicious intentions?"

Wickham gave Darcy a sinister, cold-hearted stare. He studied his fingers and then glared at his former friend. He leaned forward in his seat. "Tell me this, Darcy ... why not her?"

Chapter 16

A Little Mistaken

Weeks later, Mrs. Bennet was sitting alone and feeling forlorn, for her Lydia had departed for Newcastle with her husband the prior day, when a loud disturbance in the hallway interrupted her reverie. An older woman with a haughty, noble mien stormed into the room with Mr. William Collins trailing close behind her, thus granting Mrs. Bennet the sole privilege of receiving her. The tall, heavy-looking young man was a mixture of contrition and excitement. He went directly to the lady of the house and bowed deeply. "I beg your pardon, Mrs. Bennet. I wish to acquaint you with my noble patroness, Lady Catherine de Bourgh."

Mrs. Bennet promptly stood and dropped a curtsy. "Oh! This is such an honour to receive you, your ladyship. Mr. Collins speaks exceedingly well of your benevolence."

Her ladyship's countenance contorted with disdain. "This is not a social call. I am here for a single purpose of which you can be at no loss to understand."

"Why, I would have supposed you were in the vicinity, and you meant to convey word of how Mr. and Mrs. Collins are getting along. Yet, as Mr. Collins is here, I can only suppose that his wife, Charlotte, is visiting her family at Lucas Lodge. I suppose she thinks too highly of herself to call on Longbourn out of fear that she might be distracted with notions of all the many changes she wishes to make once my dear husband departs this earth. Wishing to ascertain the condition of the estate, you decided you would call on Longbourn for yourself."

Lady Catherine's mouth gaped. "Nothing in your ridiculous ramblings has anything to do with my purpose in being here. My nephew Fitzwilliam Darcy is foolish enough to suppose he is in love with your daughter Miss Elizabeth Bennet. I have come here to persuade the young lady to think better of my nephew's scheme to offer his hand in marriage."

Hearing only that which she wanted to hear, Mrs. Bennet's face ignited with elation. "Mr. Darcy and Lizzy are to be married?" She placed her hand on her bosom. "Two daughters married to such handsome gentlemen! I shall go distracted. Oh! Wait until I share my happy news with all my friends and neighbours. Did you know that Mr. Darcy has ten thousand a year? My Lizzy will be so very rich, and she will have many fine carriages and such pin money. She will have no need for Lady Barrett's fortune now. Oh! And she will put her other sisters in the path of many rich gentlemen."

She covered her mouth with her handkerchief to calm her nerves. "My God! We are saved." Mrs. Bennet glared at Mr. Collins and jutted her chin. "You and your scheming wife are welcome to Longbourn. I can imagine it is nothing to Pemberley."

"Do not get ahead of yourself! I merely mentioned my nephew's plans. Nothing has been decided, and nothing will be decided if I have a say. That is the purpose in my being here. I insist upon seeing Miss Bennet this instant."

"Then your ladyship will be quite disappointed."

"Nonsense—I am not in the habit of brokering disappointment. Summon your daughter at once!"

"I wish that I could, for we have much planning to do if we are to have a proper wedding. However, Lizzy is not here."

"Where on earth is she if she is not here?"

"My daughter has travelled to visit her aunt."

Enraged in having missed Elizabeth, Lady Catherine headed straight to the door without taking a proper leave of Mrs. Bennet. Her faithful servant trailed along behind her. She insisted that Mrs. Bennet deserved no consideration after having wasted so much of her precious time. Her ladyship was gone as quickly as she had come, leaving Mrs. Bennet in quite a state.

Elizabeth, in fact, had begun her journey of only twenty-four miles early that morning. How she had missed her Uncle and Aunt Gardiner since she last saw them at Longbourn this past December. Several years had passed since she and her sister Jane were last in Cheapside. Her being in the Gardiners' home after so long a time was a painful reminder that her dearest Jane would never pass through those hallways again. Elizabeth knew that if she allowed herself to dwell on such matters for long, then she might not possess the courage to accomplish what she meant to during the visit.

Her aunt eagerly welcomed Elizabeth in the drawing room. Mrs. Gardiner was an amiable, intelligent, elegant woman and a great favourite with all her Longbourn nieces. With Elizabeth, there was a particular regard. There was so much to tell, and they spoke on many subjects with alacrity, though none of it as seriously as the matter of Lydia's elopement.

"I am surprised your father consented to the newlyweds calling at Longbourn before taking their leave to Newcastle, not to mention their staying an entire week, after the way the marriage came about."

"As scandalous as it was, it is so fortunate that Lydia was married in Gretna Green, but wait until you hear what I need to tell you.

"It appears my family's good fortune is all due to a gentleman named Mr. Darcy."

"Mr. Darcy? Would this be Mr. Darcy of Pemberley and Derbyshire?"

"Yes. How do you know of him?"

"You will recall my having spoken of growing up in Lambton. It is a small town but five miles from Pemberley. The larger question is how does Lydia know Mr. Darcy?"

"She did not. The day he *called* on her, as she so foolishly asserts, was the first time she ever laid eyes on him.

"Lydia said that she did not think they would ever make it to Gretna Green, and it was a good thing Mr. Darcy called on them; otherwise, she suspected she and Wickham might not be married still. Mind you, she had not intended to tell me because it was meant to be a secret, but once she inadvertently mentioned Mr. Darcy's being in Gretna Green, I would not let it rest until I knew the full account."

Elizabeth had heard such a jumbled mixture of ridiculousness from her youngest sister as to be exceedingly puzzled. She uttered foolish ramblings of having had a rivalry for *her* Wickham's affection with Mr. Darcy's sister and having emerged the victor. Lydia continued on about how she was much prettier than the other young lady, for her Wickham had always told her so.

What on earth did Mr. Wickham have to do with Miss Darcy? Whatever it was, could it have been the impetus for Mr. Darcy's strong dislike of the man? None of this was anything she might share with her aunt. For all Elizabeth knew, her sister may have contrived the entire story—not without some encouragement from that husband of hers. Elizabeth simply detested the man after his despicable behaviour towards her youngest sister— even if she was obliged to refer to him as her brother forever more.

"It would then appear that we all owe Mr. Darcy a debt of gratitude."

"Indeed. I do not get on one bit with the notion of Mr. Darcy taking so much upon himself. I know Mr. Wickham and Mr. Darcy have been acquainted since their youth." Elizabeth shrugged. "I do not know much about their history except to say that Mr. Darcy abhors the gentleman."

"How do you know how Mr. Darcy feels about Mr. Wickham? Lizzy, have you an acquaintance with the gentleman that you have yet to confide in me?"

"Oh, dearest Aunt Gardiner, if you only knew."

"I have all day."

Elizabeth commenced telling her aunt all there was to tell about her acquaintance with Mr. Darcy. The only question in her mind was why he had gone to such lengths on behalf of her family. *Surely the endeavour could not have been very pleasant for him.*

"It seems to me you know perfectly well why the gentleman behaved as he did. My question is why will you not admit it?"

"I am afraid to allow myself to hope. I believe I treated him abominably when attempting to persuade him of my indifference: first in Bosley when I refused to give him the assurances that I would remain there and wait for his return and again in Hertfordshire when I spurned his offer to be of service to my family in Lydia's recovery. While he proclaims to be a patient man, I fear I may have exhausted him."

"Why do you say that? You will concede that neither of your attempts served as a sufficient deterrent. When you did not await his return in Bosley, he came to you in Hertfordshire.

When you tried to persuade him that his assistance was not required, he took it wholly upon himself to recover Lydia and at considerable expense, I would imagine."

"Yes, but it has been weeks since Lydia and Wickham were married. Mr. Darcy must find the idea of aligning himself with the Wickhams an abomination, or else he would have returned to Hertfordshire by now."

"From all I know of the gentleman and even by your own account, Mr. Darcy is a rich and powerful man. Have you allowed for the possibility that he has obligations and responsibilities that make it impossible for him to return to Hertfordshire at this time?"

"For once, I have decided against rushing to judgment, hence my presence in Town. If I could see him, then I would be able to judge for myself if he still holds me in esteem or if the promises he made were nothing more than words—words erased by the brush of scandal."

"My dear, if you have come to London as a means of putting yourself in Mr. Darcy's path, then I am afraid I will not be of much service to you. We live in very different parts of town. All our connections are so different. As you well know, we go out so little that it is very improbable that you should meet at all, unless it is made known to him that you are in Town, and he comes to see you."

"Actually, I have taken matters into my own hands in that regard. I have written the young lady I met in Bosley when I was staying with my aunt Lady Vanessa Barrett. She and Mr. Darcy have connections which are very much the same. She remains in Town. I shall call on her tomorrow."

The next day found Elizabeth in a fashionable Mayfair establishment visiting her friend. Elizabeth and Lucy sat upon the latter's canopied bed, just as had been their wont in Bosley. Months had passed since they last saw each other, but time had done nothing to diminish their affection for each other, likely a consequence of their frequent letters as well as the ladies' understanding of the inner workings of each other's heart.

Elizabeth said, "I always supposed Lord Holland and you would make an excellent match, Lucy. You are so much alike in temperament."

"I could not agree more. Alas, my parents have deigned I am to marry Mr. Franklin Lloyd. I am obliged to honour their wishes." Lucy took both of Elizabeth's hands in hers. "I envy you in being free from such restrictions. I truly do."

"Whatever do you mean?"

"Surely you are no stranger to the fact that Lady Vanessa and Lady Clarissa intended you for Lord Holland."

"Close to the end of my stay in Bosley, I suspected as much, but I began to consider it rather a fond wish rather than anything more compelling."

"Nevertheless, you follow your own counsel when it comes to matters of the heart. Otherwise, we might never have met. You would be known as Mrs. Elizabeth Collins, and you would be residing in Kent as the wife of a parson."

Elizabeth laughed at this image of herself. "Perish the thought, dear Lucy." She could not believe she had confided in Lucy the awkward embarrassment she endured in rejecting her ridiculous cousin's hand in marriage.

"I wish very much that Mr. Darcy had not been so obtuse. The two of you might have—" Lucy sucked in a quick breath. "Oh, Elizabeth, I am so sorry to touch upon what must surely be a sore subject. I am not unaware of his being the reason you went away from Bosley."

"Lucy, you need not worry ever much over me. I suppose I should have mentioned before that I have since seen Mr. Darcy."

"You have? Well, that is wonderful news. Is it not?"

"I suppose that depends. You will recall meeting his friend Charles Bingley."

"Yes, he was a delightful man and so very handsome. But his sister—" Lucy turned up her nose in a manner eerily reminiscent of Caroline Bingley herself. "Wherever did she come from?"

"Caroline Bingley does leave much to be desired. She is nothing compared to her brother, for he is one hundred times her worth. However, I mentioned Mr. Bingley because his estate in Hertfordshire is next to my father's estate. Mr. Darcy was recently in residence there."

"That is wonderful. Surely he came all that way to see you. What other purpose would he have in Hertfordshire? Did the two of you reach an understanding?"

"I am afraid we did not. There was hardly any time. He left Hertfordshire rather hastily for matters I have come to learn were of grave importance."

"Oh! I have a wonderful idea! I understand Mr. Darcy is in Town, both he and Lord Holland, and you know his lordship rarely ventures to London if he can help it. I expect the two of them will be at the Langley's garden party tomorrow. You should accompany me. My mother shall have no problem securing an extra invitation. Lord Holland, Mr. Darcy, you, and I will be together again just as we were in Bosley. We shall have a gay reunion."

Chapter 17

Half Agony, Half Hope

The prospect of Mr. Darcy standing there, bestowing his undivided attention on another filled Elizabeth with unrest. She lowered her voice and leaned closer to her friend. "Who is that striking young woman in Mr. Darcy's company?" Indeed, Mr. Darcy's companion was tall, and her appearance was womanly and graceful. She had Elizabeth seeing green.

Lucy turned to command a better view of the couple. "I have no idea of who she might be. While this is not my first Season, this is the first I have ever seen of her. She is lovely."

"Indeed, she is. Is there any wonder that he hangs upon that woman's every word?"

Still studying the couple, Lucy tapped her fingers against her chin. "However, she is rather young for a gentleman of his discerning taste, do you not agree?"

Elizabeth's mind wandered to her own sister. The disparity in Lydia and Mr. Wickham's age did not serve as a deterrent to the lieutenant. She shook her head to ward off her musings. *Mr. Wickham and Mr. Darcy are leagues apart.* Still, she could not help being concerned. *Regardless of her age, the young woman is completely enamoured of Mr. Darcy.*

"Elizabeth, what are we waiting for? Let us go over and ascertain who she is."

"Heaven forbid, Lucy! I shall do no such thing."

"Then I shall go. Wait here. I shall report back as soon as I know the particulars."

Before Elizabeth could stop her friend, Lucy had set off in Mr. Darcy's direction. Deciding to spare herself the pain of knowing more about Mr. Darcy's companion, Elizabeth hurried off in the opposite direction. She needed time alone to think—to dwell on those matters that must surely increase her current sufferings.

She wandered about in the garden until she came across a place to sit. Elizabeth buried her face in her hands. *Why did I come? Despite what Mr. Darcy did for Lydia, I believe the confluence of wretched occurrences when last we were together was too much for a relationship as tenuous as ours to endure.*

There was no mistaking in her mind that whoever the young woman was, she was important to him. In all the time she had occasion to observe him in company, she had never seen him regard anyone with so much affection. Elizabeth's heart sank. *Is he lost to me?*

Elizabeth covered her face with both hands. *Here I go again, rushing to conclusions. Better I walk right up to Mr. Darcy and make my presence known. Pray that companion of his has found another means of diversion by now.* Elizabeth's spirits rallied. She stood straight and tall. *I have travelled this far so that I might determine the present workings of Mr. Darcy's heart. I shall not turn back now.*

Lord Holland passed by Darcy on the steps leading to the balcony. He nodded. "Where is Miss Bennet?"

"I beg your pardon?"

"Miss Bennet. I had expected the two of you to have been inseparable once you learned of her presence."

"The last I saw of Miss Bennet, we were in Hertfordshire. That was weeks ago. Do you mean to say she is now in London?"

"Not only is she in London, but she is here."

How can that be? Surely Elizabeth would not be here, and I have been completely unaware of it. I wonder if she knows of my presence. If so, why has she not sought me out? Unless—

"Pardon me." Darcy walked away from his friend with the speed of lightning. *If she is here, then I must find her.* He looked inside the house and out, and finally, he ventured into the garden.

Emerging from opposite sides of a towering rosebush, the two nearly collided into each other.

"Eliza—" He clasped his hands behind his back to keep himself from reaching out and touching her as was his wont in his dreams. "I had no indication you were in Town."

Elizabeth was in the midst of rehearsing the speech she planned to make when she found him and thus failed to attend to those courtesies expected upon seeing him after so long a time. "Mr. Darcy! I am staying with my aunt and uncle in Cheapside. I came to the party as Lucy's guest."

"Ah, Miss Lancaster! I believe I saw her earlier."

"She and I both saw you. I might add that you seemed quite enraptured with your companion."

"You saw me, and you failed to make your presence known? Why did you not speak to me? I might have introduced you to my *companion.*"

"Do you suppose I am the sort of female who puts herself in the path of a gentleman in heated pursuit of another woman?"

"If you suppose that I was in *heated pursuit* of another woman, then surely you do not know me. In fact, I readily concede that there is much that we do not know about each other. What I do know is that you, Miss Elizabeth Bennet, are the most bewildering woman I have ever met. That you would continue to doubt my constancy is beyond comprehension."

"What am I to think? You and I did not part under the most favourable circumstances, sir."

"About that—there is a matter that I need to discuss with you. I fully intended to return to Hertfordshire, once my business in Town was completed."

"If you are about to tell me what you did for my sister Lydia, I already know."

"I might have known Mrs. Wickham was not to be trusted to keep such matters to herself."

"I am glad she told me; otherwise, I would not have been able to thank you on behalf of my family."

"If you will thank me," he replied, "let it be for yourself alone. Much as I respect your family, I believe I thought only of you."

Elizabeth was too much embarrassed to say a word. She simply smiled.

Their intimate discourse drew the attention of every passerby, who must surely have pondered the identity of Mr. Darcy's companion. He reached for Elizabeth's hand, placed it over his arm, and led her to a secluded spot inside an ivy covered gazebo.

"Mr. Darcy, what will people say should they discover the two of us tucked away here?"

"Let them say what they will. Have I not pledged thee my troth?" He retrieved a golden locket from his breast pocket. "I am yours. I always have been yours. You need only trust that.

"From the moment you bestowed this upon me, I felt myself to be as solemnly engaged to you as if the strictest legal covenant had bound us to each other."

Elizabeth stepped closer and captured the locket in her hand. A lock of her own hair was bound with gold thread and encased inside. She read the inscription on the other side. "A lasting love affair." *How sweet the sound.* She felt the colour spread over her body. Even during the earliest days of their acquaintance, he was intent upon loving her.

Darcy said, "Do you remember our first kiss?"

Elizabeth said nothing.

"I shall always remember our first kiss, and I am rather certain the same goes for you. However, in case I am mistaken, in case you do not recall our first kiss as clearly as if it were this morning, I would like to remind you." Darcy glided his fingers along her chin. "May I?"

The look in her eyes was all the encouragement he needed. He claimed her lips. Her soft moan recalled him to their surroundings, and he ceased. Still, he did not relinquish his touch upon her face. He gazed into her eyes and smiled. "I knew I was in trouble the first time I laid eyes on you. Your manner of walk, the liveliness of your mind—I have never been as bewitched by any woman as I am by you. I adore you. I love you. Marry me, Elizabeth."

"Marry you, Mr. Darcy?"

"Please. Be my wife, and come live with me at Pemberley." In case she was prepared to be stubborn, Darcy lowered himself on bended knee.

"Mr. Darcy, what are you doing? Please return to your feet at once before someone happens upon us."

"I intend to remain in this attitude until you say yes."

"Yes, I will marry you. Does that make you happy?"

"Indeed, you have made me the happiest man in the world."

Darcy stood. He moved his hands along either side of her long, slender neckline, leaned in, and kissed her upon her lips ... lightly at first and then slowly coaxed them apart. Kissing the woman he loved like this took his breath away and filled his body with longing. Wanting more than their situation afforded, he slowly ceased. Pulling away, he smoothed his thumb over Elizabeth's sweet puckered lips.

He captured her hand in his. "Come with me. I should like very much to introduce you to my *companion*."

"There is no need to do that, sir. I am quite satisfied not knowing any of your other female admirers."

"But you will want to meet this particular admirer, for she is to be your sister."

"Mr. Darcy! How dare you allow me to go on as I did earlier?"

"Pray you will forgive me, but I have never seen you show signs of jealousy. I rather enjoyed the prospect."

"Indeed, I was jealous ... and rather foolish. Can you forgive me?"

He brushed a kiss atop her knuckles. "Always, my love—always."

Darcy and Elizabeth found his sister inside the house, sitting with an elderly woman, no doubt her companion, Mrs. Annesley. The young lady did not look nearly as animated as she had earlier. She sprang from her seat and headed her brother's way when she espied him entering the room. From her talks with Mr. Darcy about his younger sister, Elizabeth knew she was little more than sixteen. Her figure was formed, giving Elizabeth the earlier impression of her being older. Elizabeth considered this a sufficient excuse for not realising whom the young woman was earlier. She was less handsome than her brother, but upon closer inspection, Elizabeth discerned the similarities in the siblings' countenances.

"Georgiana, meet Miss Elizabeth Bennet. Miss Bennet, this is my sister."

Georgiana, whose manners were perfectly unassuming and gentle, curtsied. "Miss Bennet, it is such a pleasure finally to meet you. My brother speaks very highly of you."

"Miss Darcy, the pleasure is all mine. Your brother has told me so much about you. He says you are a very accomplished pianist. I hope to enjoy the honour of hearing you play."

"I should like that very much."

Wanting to share the happy occasion with his sister, Darcy looked at Elizabeth and silently begged the question. Elizabeth nodded.

Darcy said, "I have news that I trust will please you, Georgiana. You and Miss Bennet shall have ample opportunity to enjoy performing on the pianoforte—at Pemberley."

Georgiana arched her brow and looked at both Elizabeth and Darcy. "Are you planning to visit Pemberley, Miss Bennet? How wonderful!"

"Indeed, Miss Bennet will be travelling with us to Derbyshire as soon as certain arrangements can be made; however, she will not be travelling as Miss Bennet, but as Mrs. Darcy."

Georgiana's mouth gaped.

"You are the first to know. I asked Miss Bennet to be my wife, and she said yes."

The young lady found her voice. "Fitzwilliam, Miss Bennet, this is wonderful news." She embraced Elizabeth. "We shall be sisters!"

"Indeed, and I should like nothing more than if you call me by my given name—Elizabeth or Lizzy, whichever you prefer."

"I would be honoured, and you must call me Georgiana."

Soon, Lucy joined the happy gathering. "Elizabeth, where did you go? I have been looking all over for you. I see you have been introduced to Miss Darcy."

Darcy bowed slightly and said, "Miss Lancaster, it is a pleasure to see you again."

Lucy realised her lapse in decorum and curtsied. "Oh, where are my manners? It is a pleasure seeing you, too, Mr. Darcy."

"I take it you know who my sister is."

Lucy threw Elizabeth a perplexed grimace and looked back at Darcy. "I – I saw you two earlier, and I took it upon myself to make inquiries."

Darcy reached out his hand. "There is no need to explain. Allow me to introduce you properly. Miss Lancaster, this is my sister, Miss Darcy. Georgiana, meet Miss Lancaster."

After the young ladies had greeted each other genially, Lucy turned to Elizabeth. "You are looking rather pleased—in fact you are beaming." She then directed her gaze to Mr. Darcy. "And I do not know when I have ever seen you smiling so brightly. Has something happened that I should know about?"

Elizabeth looked at Darcy for confirmation to share the happy news. He nodded. "Mr. Darcy and I are to be married."

Lucy's smile could hardly be contained as she embraced Elizabeth. "Married! I always knew this day would come. You must invite me to the wedding. In fact, I should like to be your maid of honour." Lucy pulled back and spoke to Darcy. "You should ask Lord Holland to be your groomsman!"

Elizabeth said, "Please, Lucy, we have only been engaged for an hour. We have hardly had time to consider the wedding ceremony!"

Lord Holland soon wandered into the parlour. As if unable to stop herself, Lucy called out to him from across the room, and she beckoned he join her party with a wave of her hand.

Having spoken to Elizabeth and Lucy earlier, he held his hand out to Georgiana. Upon accepting hers, he bowed slightly. "Miss Darcy, it is a pleasure to see you again." Georgiana demurred under his attention and acknowledged his gesture in a voice barely above a whisper.

Releasing her hand, he turned to Darcy. "I see you found Miss Bennet."

Lucy said, "I should say so, and wait until you hear their happy news."

By the turn of Darcy's countenance, Lucy had spoken out of turn, but that was her way. Lord Holland had to find out somehow, and it might as well have been that instant as any other time.

He looked at his friend expectantly.

Darcy cleared his throat "Miss Bennet has agreed to marry me."

Lord Holland glanced at Elizabeth's face and detected a certain air that was not there when he saw her earlier that afternoon. "The two of you have my ardent wishes for happiness." Speaking to Darcy, he said, "I would say this calls for a toast. Will you join me?"

Darcy really wanted to steal away with Elizabeth and spend the rest of the day as well as the evening basking in the glow of their shared felicity, but decorum would not allow for such a pleasurable endeavour. She had come to the garden party as Miss Lancaster's guest. Surely she would be obliged to leave with her, and who was to say how long the Lancasters would remain at the gathering.

Elizabeth said, "Miss Darcy, perhaps you will join Lucy and me for a glass of punch." Georgiana agreed and with that the ladies went away, thus affording the gentlemen privacy.

Lord Holland said, "It seems your persistence paid off, my friend."

Darcy nodded. "As I told you in Bosley, Miss Bennet means everything to me."

"Indeed you did, and I am not unaware how much you have long meant to her. Again, I congratulate you."

"It means a great deal to hear you say that. I know you care for her as well."

"It is true; I care for her as I always will, for we are connected. We share unbreakable ties through Lady Vanessa. Then, too, there is *our* shared interest. I suppose the next time you are in Bosley, you will be married and no doubt will be staying at Barrington Hall, but you must know you are always welcome to stay at Avondale should you wish."

"I hope your generous offer extends to my cousin Colonel Fitzwilliam as well."

"Why do you say that?"

"He will oversee my interests. I have spent far too much time away from Derbyshire over the past five years pursuing my passion for horse racing. Once I take my bride to Pemberley, I believe it will be a long time before I am persuaded to go away."

Days later, a loud disturbance in the hallway impeded upon Lady Vanessa's felicity. She nearly dropped her fine porcelain cup on the floor when the butler stepped aside and in stormed Lady Catherine de Bourgh. Seeing no cause for civility given the manner of Lady Catherine's entrance, Lady Vanessa did not invite her guest to be seated. "What on earth have I done to deserve a second visit? Did we not say all there was to say when you were here before? What are you doing here?"

Lady Catherine rested both hands on her walking stick. "Unlike you, I am not so easily dissuaded. I went to Hertfordshire to confront this Miss Elizabeth Bennet, only to be told that she had travelled to visit her aunt. Are you not her aunt? I insist upon seeing the young woman this instant."

Lady Vanessa shook her head. "It is a shame you have travelled all this way. Of course, I am Elizabeth's aunt, as you well know. However, I am not her *only* aunt. If you had taken the time to ask, you might have realised that."

The haughty aristocrat sucked in a quick breath. "Do you mean to say Miss Bennet is not here? Do you mean to say that I have travelled all this way to carry my point for naught?"

"That is precisely what I am saying." Lady Vanessa pursed her lips and studied her guest for a moment. "Do you not consider that it is time to give up the fight? The last time I saw your nephew was in this very room, and I will have you know that he was a most determined young man. He would not relent until I handed him a letter of introduction to my brother, and therein, I gave my brother assurances that I was fully in support of a possible alliance between Mr. Darcy and my niece if that was indeed her wish.

"If what you say of Elizabeth visiting her aunt is true, then she will be in London. I have it on good authority that Mr. Darcy is in London as well. It is highly probable that the two have come to an understanding."

Lady Catherine huffed. "It is no wonder that you would be in favour of the match. My nephew's fortune is splendid. Your own fortune is nothing in comparison. An alliance with my nephew can only raise the entire Bennet family's standing, and that includes you. Alas, what of my nephew? You must know that Miss Bennet's youngest sister—your own niece—was recently married to the son of the late Mr. Darcy's steward. Is such a man to be brother to my nephew? Are the shades of Pemberley to be thus polluted?"

Lady Vanessa continued eyeing Lady Catherine with circumspect. The latter was nowhere near as robust and steady as when she first came to Bosley. Lady Vanessa could do no less than to regard her with a measure of compassion. "You look rather peaked, your ladyship. Please have a seat, and take tea with me. Then you must consider staying here at Barrington Hall—at least for the night. Perhaps I might summon the physician to have a look at you. One can never be too careful once one reaches a certain age."

"I shall do no such thing. Do you suppose that I do not know exactly what is afoot by your sudden show of concern for my health? You mean to delay my departure for London." She turned and headed for the door. "I shall not be detained. I mean to carry my point."

Chapter 18

In Favour of Matrimony

One month later, and with a delightfully short season of courtship behind her, Mrs. Elizabeth Darcy paused a moment to reflect upon all her good fortune and the joy she felt in being surrounded by family, friends, and acquaintances at the wedding breakfast. What a relief it had been to be married by special license. Though her husband was often subjected to the absurdities of her mother, her sisters, and occasionally her own father, he bore it with admirable calm.

Upon hearing of the engagement from Elizabeth herself, Mrs. Bennet was a mixture of amazement and contentment. It was just as Lady Catherine had foretold, and thus Mrs. Bennet could not be too surprised when her Lizzy confirmed the veracity of her ladyship's claim, even if they was a bit premature. Mrs. Bennet had already taught herself to think exceedingly fond of Mr. Darcy—having entertained him for dinner. His acknowledgment that the partridges were remarkably well done was a cause for quite a bit of boasting to her neighbours, for, after all, he was a man of ten thousand pounds a year. She was doubly pleased that her scheme for Kitty to turn the gentleman's head did not unfold, for Lizzy's nuptials had been the means of his friend Bingley finally returning to Hertfordshire— a very single Mr. Bingley.

Bingley, Elizabeth observed, was standing alone by the hearth nodding and smiling at many of the guests as they passed by. He looked as though the most significant part of him were missing. Elizabeth could well imagine her beloved sister Jane by his side. She sighed. *Perhaps in another place and time.*

Never did Elizabeth expect that the Bingley sisters would deign to attend the nuptials. She supposed Miss Bingley must surely be deeply mortified by Mr. Darcy's marriage—its being the means of forever thwarting her intention of being the next mistress of Pemberley. Elizabeth surmised Caroline had dropped all her resentment and even attempted to pay off every arrear of civility as a means of retaining the right of visiting at Pemberley.

Elizabeth's two closest friends from Bosley were present as well. Anyone who paid any attention at all to Lucy and Lord Holland would have mistaken them as a couple. How Elizabeth wished that might one day be the case. Even now, she had not abandoned her intention of seeing it so.

As pleased as she was to see Georgiana standing across the room speaking with Colonel Fitzwilliam, Elizabeth would have wished to see more of Mr. Darcy's relations at the wedding. She had met his aunt and uncle Lord and Lady Matlock as well as the viscount, Lord Robert Fitzwilliam, during her stay in Town. The two people she was most curious about, Lady Catherine de Bourgh and her daughter, Anne, also did not come. The former did, however, write her nephew a very long letter, but he did not share its contents with his bride. He would only mention his aunt's complaints that what had started as a trifling cold had manifested itself into a malady far more inconvenient. *A conse-*

quence of her extensive and by now well publicised travels, Elizabeth surmised.

She was gratified by the easy attachment forming between her sisters Mary and Kitty with Georgiana. She could well imagine the three of them becoming fast friends. As for her youngest sister, Mrs. Wickham, already, Elizabeth had received several letters detailing the hardships that she faced in Newcastle. She further affirmed that now that her sister was so very rich, Elizabeth should consider extending them a helping hand with a mere three or four hundred pounds now and again—a small sum indeed for a sister whose husband had ten thousand pounds a year. Elizabeth, having exacted the full account of her husband's ardent dislike of George Wickham and why he insisted that the man never be allowed to visit Pemberley, appreciated even more the extent of his sacrifice in saving her sister from utter disgrace, and she honoured him even more.

Elizabeth was happy to see her Aunt and Uncle Gardiner in conversation with her husband and happier still that her dear aunt thought nearly as highly of him as Elizabeth did. *There is something of dignity in his countenance that gives one a favourable idea of his heart,* was the sentiment avowed by Mrs. Gardiner when congratulating her niece on the nuptials. It warmed Elizabeth's heart to hear the aunt, who would always be her favourite, speak in such a manner about her husband. She could hardly wait to receive the Gardiners at Pemberley.

Nothing warmed Elizabeth's heart more than seeing her father and Lady Vanessa reunited after so many long years of estrangement. Her ladyship, if she would admit it, truly enjoyed returning to her childhood home. Upon designating Elizabeth her sole heir, Lady Vanessa's standing increased one-hundred fold amongst the Bennets of Longbourn.

Being a future heiress was well and good, Elizabeth considered, but that was far from what endeared her ladyship to her niece. That commendation was earned with Lady Vanessa's having invited Elizabeth to live with her in Bosley and thereby providing the means of uniting her with the best man in the world.

From the moment she had first laid eyes on her new home, Elizabeth was struck with the notion that being the mistress of Pemberley was truly something. All that she saw and admired upon seeing Pemberley for the first time had formed a fond impression upon her memory, and she often reflected on the moment. The park was very large and contained a great variety of ground. They had driven for some time through a beautiful wood stretching over a wide extent and gradually ascended for half-a-mile. They then found themselves at the top of a considerable eminence where the wood ceased and Pemberley House, situated on the opposite side of a valley, instantly caught the eye. She gasped upon espying the large, handsome stone building which stood well on rising ground and was backed by a ridge of high woody hills. A stream of some natural importance flowed in front. Its banks were neither formal nor falsely adorned. Elizabeth was delighted. She had never seen a place for which nature had done more or where natural beauty had been so little counteracted by an awkward taste.

Elizabeth had finished the last of her letters to her family, and thanks to Betsy, they were placed in the downstairs tray for posting. She was now at leisure to commit her fondest thoughts on the happenings at Pemberley to her journal. It had been some time since she learned to think of her frequent writings as such, as opposed to letters meant for her beloved Jane. Elizabeth owed it to Betsy's unrelenting persistence to know for whom the letters were meant as well as her subsequent understanding once she discovered their true purpose. No one was more surprised than Betsy, herself, when Elizabeth prevailed upon Lady Vanessa to allow Betsy to come to Pemberley and be Elizabeth's lady's maid.

Elizabeth opened her drawer, took out her gold brooch, and unfastened it. Just over two years ago when she was holding her beloved sister as she drew her last breath, Elizabeth never could have imagined such a life as this: a beautiful home and a loving husband. She also had the means of raising her family's lot in life as the future heiress of the Barrett fortune. How glad she was that she finally took a chance and opened her heart to all that life afforded. *As I look at where I am and all that I have, I can have no cause to complain.*

Deciding that her journal entry could wait, Elizabeth placed the brooch that she had worn nearly every day for the past two years back in the drawer. She walked over to the window seat and drew in a deep breath as the sun's warmth washed over her face. Once settled comfortably in the window seat, Elizabeth reflected on how far she had come in so short a period of time.

I never dreamed it possible to feel such happiness and contentment ever again. She reached into her pocket and retrieved her new locket. Smiling, she considered what it meant to her. Moments later, when she espied her husband entering the room, she clutched the locket in her hand and folded her arm behind her back.

He sat next to her and kissed her gently on her cheek. "You are being very mysterious, my love. What are you hiding?"

"You might say it is a present of sorts."

"A present for me? You need not to have gone to the trouble."

"Actually, it is a gift that I intended for myself, although I confess I would never have procured it were it not for you."

"This is mysterious. May I ask what it is?"

"I shall show you." She removed her hand from behind her back and opened it to reveal the locket.

Darcy touched his breast pocket and assured himself that nothing was amiss. "It is a perfect replica of my own." He took

Elizabeth's locket in his hand, opened it, and proceeded to admire it. He ran his free hand through his hair. "When did you manage this?" Darcy asked as he examined the contents.

"You will recall succumbing to slumber in the carriage ride to London after our wedding breakfast."

He ran his fingers through his hair again, this time more slowly as if checking to make certain it was all there. "Elizabeth, pray tell me you did not—"

Elizabeth's eyes sparkled with mischief. "Indeed, I secured a lock of your hair just as I always hoped I would one day after allowing you to have a piece of mine. Now, my love, we are even. We both shall carry a piece of each other closest to our hearts, from this day forward and for as long as we both shall live."

Darcy could do no less than grace his wife with a beautiful smile. "Two hearts entwined as one embarked upon a journey—" He claimed her in his arms, leaned in, and commenced kissing her, growing ever more urgent with each passing second and filling her completely with adoration until he took her breath away. He cradled her chin, peered deeply into her eyes, and spoke softly, "A lasting love affair."

The Author

P. O. Dixon is a writer as well as an entertainer. Historical England and its days of yore fascinate her. She, in particular, loves the Regency period with its strict mores and oh so proper decorum. Her ardent appreciation of Jane Austen's timeless works set her on the writer's journey. Dixon delights in weaving diverting tales of gallant gentlemen on horseback and the women they love. Visit podixon.com and find out more about Dixon's writing endeavors.

Connect with the Author Online

Blog: http://podixon.blogspot.com
Twitter: @podixon
Facebook: http://www.facebook.com/podixon
Pinterest: http://pinterest.com/podixon
Website: http://podixon.com
Email: podixon@podixon.com

Author's Other Books

§ Pride and Prejudice Untold Series:

- To Have His Cake (and Eat It Too): Mr. Darcy's Tale
- What He Would Not Do: Mr. Darcy's Tale Continues
- Lady Harriette: Fitzwilliam's Heart and Soul

§ Darcy and the Young Knight's Quest Series:

- He Taught Me to Hope
- The Mission: He Taught Me to Hope Christmas Vignette

Other Pride and Prejudice "What-if" Stories:

- Still a Young Man: Darcy Is In Love
- Bewitched, Body and Soul: Miss Elizabeth Bennet
- Matter of Trust: The Shades of Pemberley
- Love Will Grow: A Pride and Prejudice Story
- Only a Heartbeat Away: Pride and Prejudice Novella
- Almost Persuaded: Miss Mary King

Printed in Great Britain
by Amazon.co.uk, Ltd.,
Marston Gate.